THE *STEAM* SERIES BOOK *2*

Moonstruck

JENNIFER FISCH-FERGUSON

Editor: J. Arthur's Publishing– JAEdits.com

Cover Photo Credits: www.tri-crescent.com

Copyright © 2016 Jennifer Fisch-Ferguson

ISBN: 978-0-9911088-7-9

Table of Contents

Chapter 1

Siona Carter looked away from her computer screen and squinted at the clock on the wall. She deliberately kept it where she would need to look up to see it so she could refresh her eyes from the up close viewing of her computer screen. As she rotated her neck, her thick short coils of hair tickled her nape and she grinned. After years of not being sure just what to do with it, she had finally settled on working with the natural texture of her curls and embracing it. She grew tired of being chemically burned three or four times a year, just to keep her hair straight. Her dark hair set off equally dark brown eyes that were just big enough to look intrigued but not constantly surprised. She stood proud at five foot nine, and after seeing a terrifying video on the detriments of high heels on the foot bones, she happily switched flats.

She walked through the doors of the Hayden Planetarium and felt her heart speed up just a bit. She had been working with there for eighteen months and it still thrilled her to go to her job every day. She had loved astronomy from a young age; despite living in Manhattan and barely being able to make out the stars from the city burn. Perhaps, it would be better to say she was obsessed about the stars. She had learned to drive only because her parents reminded her that it was only a short drive away from the city to be able to see her beloved night sky. Of course it became moot point, because instead of asking for a car as a graduation gift, she had requested a telescope.

Not any little off the shelf scope, she proudly owned the Dobsian Obsession. Fifteen inches of precision-cut quality mirrors in a mounting that gave her the crispest images and lacked the distortion thinners mirrors often showed. For her it was the obvious choice of presents to receive. Prior to the telescope request, her parents had thought it a phase she was going through. Instead, Siona majored in Astrophysics and planned to go to graduate school after some research to add to her CV. Then she filled out an internship application, with no hopes of ever really making it.

The summer experience resulted in her being offered a full blown research and development job at the Hayden had been a dream come true. Granted she had only seen Dr. de Grasse Tyson a handful of times, and she doubted he knew who she was, it was still exciting to be in the same facility with the man who had made her field cool with the public masses. Though she did get tired of people asking her what she did for a living. The very long answer was that she used a lot of the principles of physics and mathematics to learn more about the universe. Her particular position was to gather data on a parameter study of the possibility of tidally triggered disc instability, which she believed could theoretically could lead to enhanced planetesimal formation in the outer regions of the protoplanetary disc and could therefore be relevant for the existence of Neptune. She was leading up to writing a scientific paper to present to the field. The short answer, how and possibly why Neptune existed.

While she loved her job, she did want to finish her degree and maybe even teach. However, it was expensive to go to graduate school and she had needed a brain break.

Seven hours later, Siona stretched and stood up. Her office remained a chilly sixty-eight degrees, which against the summer New York heat, was perfectly fine. Her computer chimed and her eyes flicked over to the screen. There was a group email reminding everyone that their secretary Lisa would be going out on maternity leave and to chip in for the party on Friday. Siona tried not to shudder, she loathed work parties. They were too loud and chaotic and she had never quite fit in. Her section of research and design collaborated with the Dish in Australia. Which meant the not-quite-but-really mandatory work parties forced her to be awake and more social at a time she was not comfortable with. She hoped that donating fifty dollars with a lame excuse would get her out of the celebration.

Her phone buzzed against her leg. She took out the phone with a slight panic. The only calls allowed through during work were from her parents. She spoke with her mother on the days containing a 'T' at eight in the morning religiously, so a call ringing in at six am made her worry. She tried to push the panic back and sound reasonably calm as she answered.

"Mom?" she asked.

"You're taking your break, yes?"

"Yes. What's wrong, Mom?" she asked.

"Nothing, Siona. I just needed to talk to you and I know you take a break now," her mother said.

Siona scaled back the panic a few notches. Her mother's voice was calm and collected. Not to mention she was right, Siona's break schedule was absolutely predictable. Then again, why not wait to call at eight?

"Okay, did you have a problem sleeping?"

"Oh, my worried child, relax. I am often up at six a.m. retired or not, it's hard to break a thirty year work habit of getting up early."

Siona nodded at the phone and grabbed her Bluetooth. Usually her six a.m. break meant grabbing an apple or pear, and walking twenty laps around her department. Twenty laps was exactly a mile, and with all the sitting she did on a nightly basis Siona was determined not to have varicose veins at a young age. She grimaced as she figured the eating part of her routine would have to wait. She left her office and began her walk.

"What has you calling me so early, if it's not an emergency?" she asked.

"I wanted to let you know that we have plans this summer," her mother said.

"Oh, good. Are you and Dad going to finally take the vacation you wanted?"

"We have a family reunion this year we plan to attend," her mother said.

"Great. I think you will have a lot of fun. Are you going to drive or fly?"

"We plan to drive; you still have three weeks of unused vacation, right?"

Siona almost tripped as her mother's question caught up with her. She was glad for the empty corridor to spare her the embarrassment and continued on her walk.

"What does my accrued vacation time have anything to do with your vacation?" she asked cautiously.

"Siona. Did you miss the part where I said we were going to a family reunion?"

"Oh, you mean *we,* as in the whole family," Siona said flatly.

"And this is why you graduated with honors," her mother quipped.

"Thanks Mom," Siona said drily. "When is the blessed event?"

"August, I gave you three months' notice," her mother said.

Siona could picture the smug smile her mother wore on the other end. As she ran through a list of excuses, she realized there weren't any. As her mother well knew, she had not actually taken a leave since starting her job. The Hayden was more than generous with time off for her department; however, Siona hadn't taken used the days because she saw no need. Her job fascinated her and she loved what she did. She had apparently made a huge mistake in telling her mother about the vacation time- since now it was being used against her.

"August, okay. If you can just text me the dates, I will put in my request."

"Don't sound so excited, Si," her mother laughed. "You have enjoyed the family reunions so far. It's been four years since our last visit, so it's time."

Siona again nodded to the empty hall. Despite being an only child and used to peace and quiet, she had found her extended family to be warm and welcoming when they had gone before. There would be music, storytelling, more food than the imagination could conjure and hordes of family members. The family reunions always spanned the better part of two weeks and alternated between a northern and southern location every two years.

"Where are we at this year?

"Burton, Michigan."

"Oh, I should have figured. How long has it been since you've been home, Mom?" Siona asked.

Her memories of her mother's hometown were pretty vague. The most she knew is that it was a factory city. The freeways seemed to go on forever, but the good part was no traffic. And the donuts; even after eight years Siona's mouth watered with the remembrance of the nutty donuts and made a mental note to ask her mother about the place. She continued to chat with her mom for her twenty minute break and promised to have her vacation request turned in before she left.

Siona went back to her lab and dove back into her work. She was deep into her numerical data when her computer chimed. Another email reminder about the baby shower for the morning crew had made its way into her mailbox. She sighed and began to close down for the day. Her phone chirped and she sighed when she saw the text from her mom. If she didn't fill out the request form, her mother had threatened to. On her way out she stopped by the HR department.

"Hey Tony," she said brightly as she walked up to the secretary.

"Hello, Siona. How was your night?" he asked.

"Fascinating as ever, but I will spare you my ramble and details you don't really want," she said with a smile.

She waited patiently as Tony took a long sip of coffee and sighed.

"See? I love that about you," he said. "You don't make me pretend to care and leave me to drink my coffee."

"You still owe me a cup from the little place on West 81st."

Being a third shift worker meant being off schedule with most of the people around her. However one thing was consistent in the Universe- coffee was the nectar of life. Tony was one of the few people who respected the differences of schedules. He grinned and waved away her reminder.

"Okay, tomorrow," he said. "Now, what can I help you with?"

"Well, here is $50 for Lisa's baby shower. When is it again?" she asked.

Tony laughed and took the money. "You've been practicing. That almost sounded like genuine interest. It's Friday at three; so sadly, you will miss the shower by a good seven hours."

Siona blessed her four day — ten hour work schedule for giving her a reprieve and tried not to look too relieved.

"Okay. I also need a vacation request form," she said.

Tony's eyebrows rose, but he said nothing as he found the appropriate form and handed it to her. She quickly scribbled out her request and turned the paper back over to him. She watched him scan it. He seemed too interested in the form.

"Thank you, Siona," he said a bit too eagerly.

"What?" she asked cautiously.

"Nothing, you're all set. I'll turn this in and you should hear back no later than end of the week," Tony said still smiling widely.

"No, there's more to it than that," her eyes narrowed. "You're grinning like Christmas just came early."

"Well, there might be a pool of bets about when or if certain staff members will use their vacation."

"So, what you are saying is there is no way this vacation request will be denied?" she asked in a forlorn tone.

"Why would you want your vacation denied?" Tony asked.

"Did you not see the reason line where I wrote 'family vacation'?" she asked.

Tony nodded and took another sip of his coffee.

"That I did, but, I also happen to know the two people who straddle your vacation dates are in HR," he said. "Go enjoy your family and remember that you get to come back to your quiet lab."

"You are no help what so ever," she grumbled. "You were supposed to save me from having to take this extended vacation."

"Where are you going? It can't possibly be that bad," he said.

"Michigan."

"And you are complaining why? Take your telescope and view the stars from a different latitude and longitude. I'm sure there might even be a planetarium or two around you to play with," Tony mocked her. "And in case you ever wondered, this is why we take bets on when you scientists will actually use your vacation time."

Siona rolled her eyes at him.

"I can really count on going?" she asked. "There is no way to get out of this?"

"Oh, yes. You are going. The pot is pretty good," he said. "I don't suppose I can talk you into talking all three weeks?"

"You plan to cut me in?"

"And promote gambling at work? I work in HR, I couldn't possibly do that," Tony said in mock outrage.

Siona gave a general sigh of disgust and was about to leave when a tall woman with perfectly coiffed hair walked into the office. Tony greeted her with enthusiasm.

"Look Kim, Siona turned in a request for vacation."

"When? Please tell me August," Kim said, shooting Siona a bright smile.

"You got it; the second and third week," Tony said. "Maybe you could convince her to take that extra week? I mean, when else is she ever going to use it?"

Siona sighed deeply at the exuberance in his voice. There was no disguising the glee coming from her co-workers and she knew her vacation would be a sure thing. She wondered if it might be possible to get a really nasty summer cold, just before the reunion which would force her to stay home.

15

"Come to Mama!" Kim said.

Siona watched in horror as Tony handed the paper over, and Kim scrawled her signature at the bottom. She then ripped off the carbon bottom and handed it to Siona.

"Have a lovely trip, Siona," she said. "I gave you the extra week anyhow."

"You two should be ashamed of yourselves," Siona muttered. "You were supposed to be my excuse not to have to go on a family vacation."

"Siona, really. Everyone needs to take a break from work," Kim said. "You have been here for eighteen months, two weeks and three days. You have never called out sick, taken any personal days, nor vacation. If it weren't against the rules, I would tell your mother you could take the entire month of August off with no problem."

"Oh yes, I'm sure my well-being is the reason for the rapid approval," Siona grumbled.

She left the office shaking her head at the laughter that followed her out the door. She walked out of the planetarium and made her way to the subway and home. Siona knew that the summer would pass rapidly fast to spite her. Fatigue hit her as soon as she sat in her favorite rocking chair.

Siona decided to forgo her morning ritual of looking at Sirius and instead crawled into bed with her ebook reader and started to read. She yawned as she reread the last paragraph; twice, then gave up and put her device down. Soon the din of the city would rise to full blown noise, and it would serve as her lullaby as she went to sleep.

Chapter 2

      Mathias Jones stared at his computer screen and pretended the construction noise didn't bother him at all. The ecstatic part of his brain reminded him that the construction was a good thing. Longway Planetarium had received a 1.5 million dollar grant to upgrade and renovate the dome as well as the rest of the interiors, which had been long overdue. The pounding headache part of his brain was sad that he still needed to work during all the mayhem. Despite his office being at the front of the building and away from the construction, the loud banging and moving of heavy objects were easily heard. He put the finishing touch into his report, attached it to an email, and sent it. The over-cautious part of him also saved it instead of just closing the document. He powered down his computer with a sigh and sat back. Being the director of educational programs was his dream job, but trying to create a summer camp schedule during the brunt of construction had been hellish.

      "Mathias, do you have a moment?"

Mathias's head snapped up to the door and met eyes with his boss Todd. He waved him in with a smile. He noticed the small wrinkle appear in Todd's forehead as he registered the sounds.

"Sure, what's up?"

"Just a few things to run by you," Todd said.

Mathias listened with rapt attention about the plans for the grand re-opening, as well the projects for the fall that would debut their new portable dome. He was thankful he had finished his summer schedule early when Todd asked for his input. The impromptu meeting lasted over two hours, but at the end he felt refreshed and invigorated about his job. The next few weeks would be chaotic to say the least, hiring new staff, training of said new staff, and preparing the reopening would consume the rest of the month. After the grand opening and all its glory, Mathias would take a two week mandatory vacation – one he knew he would need before starting his fall programs.

He left work promptly at 5 p.m. ready for some relaxation and a weekend full of fun. It was a full moon and he knew his friends would have something planned. Hoping on his bike he rode the ten miles home with ease. His roommate waved to him from the deck and threw something at him. Mathias caught the balled up piece of paper and smoothed it out.

"Guess what we are going to do tomorrow?" Nathaniel asked.

"No," he said as he crumpled the paper again and tossed it back up.

"Come on, Mathias! You have been busting your ass for weeks, what is wrong with taking a break?"

"I am not going to see some poor, exploited, college women wrestling around in a pool of jello, Nathaniel," he said.

"It's a once in a life time chance," his friend implored. "They are only here for this weekend, and then they are traveling to Ohio."

"Are Gregory and Travon going?"

The silence gave him his answer and he shook his head as he made his way to into the house and towards his room. He had been friends with Nathaniel since their fist fight in seventh grade science class. The taller lanky boy had made a rude comment about Mathias's solar system replica. The project had taken over three weeks of hard work and care. Mathias had no intention to let his passion be sneered at and had busted Nathanial's lip, twice, before the teacher made it over to them. As they sat in the principal's office waiting for their punishment he was surprised to see tears in his nemesis' eyes.

"S'up?" he had asked.

"My parents are going ship me to boarding school. They warned me about getting into another fight," the young Nathaniel had said.

"Why did you talk mess about my project then?"

"I didn't think you would fight me," the boy had said with a grin. "You're always in your science books. I figured you would be a wimp. You throw a mean punch though."

Mathias had handed him a tissue to stem the new flow of blood and they started laughing. After fifteen minutes of waiting, the principal called them into the office. Before she could reprimand them, Mathias claimed all it all to be a misunderstanding. When the principal had pressed the issue, clearly skeptical, he made up an outrageous story and ended it with the claim that they were wrestling around and meant no harm. They walked away with an appointment to see the guidance counselor and a week's worth of in-house detention, his new friend had invited him over for the weekend and they had been best friends ever since.

"Are you ready for our run tonight?" Nathaniel asked him, bringing him back to the present.

"After we visit."

He was met with a blank stare.

"It's Memorial Day weekend, so the fam is going to visit with Pops tonight," Mathias said. "You *did* plan to come and pay your respects? Or did the thoughts of girls in gelatin make you forget?"

He watched the embarrassment pass over Nathaniel's face before his friend shrugged.

"I remembered. Not to mention, I like Pops just fine. We are celebrating how he didn't die in the war, right?"

"You're an ass 'Thaniel. Now get ready to go," Mathias sighed.

"Hey, is your mom going to make those noodles I like?"

"Yes, because this party is all about your wants. I'm going to shower, be ready in twenty."

Mathias dropped his bag inside his room door, still shaking his head. Living with Nathaniel was interesting to say the least. Their "apartment" was actually the pool house behind Nathaniel's parents' home. It had three bedrooms, two bathrooms, a full kitchen and living room. It was decked out with all the comforts Mathias would probably never be able to afford. He had tried to pay rent and utilities, but was gently told that he was earning his keep by having kept Nathaniel out of jail during high school. Mathias, in general, liked the parents, but he was loyal to his friend and had never told him about that particular conversation. His musings carried him in to the shower where he reveled in the lack of construction noise. He ran through different program ideas, until an icy splash of water complete with ice cubes dumped on his head disrupted the soothing calm of his shower.

"Time's up! Pops isn't getting any younger," Nathaniel called.

Mathias bit his tongue to stem the curses that crossed his mind and turned off the water. His friend had the good sense not to be in his room as he exited the shower. He hadn't actually needed the extra jumpstart in adrenaline, and braced himself to go to his family party. He expected the usual amount of chaos, but knew if he opted not to show there would be worse problems. He dressed quickly and met his friend in the garage. He ogled the gold and black Mustang Boss 302.

"Let me drive," he said.

"Maybe you will get to drive later. I plan on having a few drinks," Nathaniel said. "Come on, we are going to be late."

Mathias barely made shut the car door before Nathaniel peeled out of the drive way. He resisted the urge to punch his friend.

Ten minutes later they arrived at his childhood home and Mathias shot his friend a heated looked. On purpose, the ride had been too fast and too careless. Pasting a tense smile on his face, he took a deep breath and walked inside. The cacophony that welcomed him brought forth an actual grin and he relaxed. Small children were playing loudly in the living room where his grandfather sat pretending to hear the television show he was watching with closed captions on. After greeting his nieces and nephews he walked over.

"Hey, Pops," he said loudly.

He placed his hand gently on the older man's arm to get his attention. He smiled at the wizened face that turned up toward him.

"Mathias, I'm so glad you could make it," his grandfather said. "How is that fancy star program of yours coming along?"

The sound of pride always boosted Mathias. He had worked hard on his degrees even though most people in his family hadn't supported that decision. The two people in his family, he could always count on were his grandparents, and they were loudly proud of his efforts.

"Real good, Pops," he said. "We just put in for another grant and at the end of this month we're having a big party for the renovations. I have special tickets for you and Granny. My boss wants to meet you."

"Good, good. We will be there. I'm not a college man like you, but I sure enjoy looking up at those stars," Pops said. "Nathaniel, how you been, son?"

"I'm fine thank you, Sir. I brought you some more of those crossword puzzle books you like."

Mathias was always surprised at the switch Nathaniel could throw. Most of the time his best friend worked at being an offensive idiot, but when it counted, he turned on the high class etiquette he had been raised with. He shook his head slightly as Nathaniel produced a good sized stack of puzzle books, in large print, and placed them on the table next to Pops chair. He also knew the respect and the affection his best friend showed to his grandparents was genuine. Despite the grumbling and mock flippancy, Nathaniel would have been hurt if the invitation to visit with his family wasn't offered each time.

"Mathias, so good to see you son."

He smiled and went to give his mother a perfunctory hug. She looked worn down and tired to him, but she always had.

"I heard you tell Pops you got a grant for the summer?"

"Yeah, no big deal. It was a private corporation so it was a lot easier," he looked around, not meeting her gaze.

"I'm real proud of you," she said.

Mathias nodded and tried to drop the conversation, but he wasn't fast enough.

"Jordan will be home in two months. It would be nice if you were here when he returns," she announced suddenly.

"I'll see, Ma. That is around the time we get ready for the next program season," he said.

"He wants to see you, Mathias. I know it's not high on your list, but you are his only brother," his mother said, her lips pressing into a thin line.

"I will try to make it. If I can't, I'll make it a point to call while he is here and have a chat with him."

Mathias walked away despite his mother trying to continue to gain a promise to see his brother. Out of his five siblings, his brother was the person he wanted to least in the world. He wished, not for the first time, that he could channel some of Nathaniel's ability to give no fucks and just leave. Instead, he pasted a smile on his face and walked through the house and into the backyard. He wanted to grab the red cup from Nathaniel's hand and down it in a gulp. Except he promised his granny many years ago that he would stay away from alcohol, so when visiting them, he did. He looked around until he found her and made his way through countless relatives over to her side.

"Why is the most beautiful woman at this party hiding over in this corner instead of dancing?"

"Oh, Mathias, no one wants to see these old bones moving around," she laughed.

"I think they have forgotten how good you are," he said.

He nodded at his cousin manning the music and then bowed to his Granny. She laughed and accepted his hand. The music changed from current pop to Sam Cooke. Mathias laughed as he watched her adopt a sassy attitude. When he had been fifteen, his Granny insisted that he learn how to do the East Coast Swing. They had spent hours together as he learned the various steps and he loved every second. He knew it had been in response to the incidents he had started to get into at school. It was her way of keeping him out of trouble and she swore he would use it someday. They moved with the lively beat and he winked at her. As the song ended, she shook her head at him.

"You tired me all out," she said.

"Granny, we both know that you can dance circles around me," Mathias said. "Thank you for indulging me."

After two hours, he was ready to call it a night and made his rounds of good-byes. Mathias had learned that a firm time limit was the best way to handle any family event. No matter how well the gatherings started, there was always a ton of alcohol. As food was consumed, at least two good fights brewed, and around the four hour mark, things escalated. He used to make excuses, but life changes had given him the perfect reason to leave, without explaining himself. His leaving early was just something everyone expected and he made his exit without incident. His friend was already seated when he made it to the car.

"You said I could drive," he said.

Nathaniel looked at him from the driver's seat and rolled his eyes.

"I said when I got drunk."
"No, you didn't. And for the record, we don't get drunk," Mathias grumbled.

"No, we don't," Nathaniel said pulling away from the curb. "Ready to run?"

The humid August air hit his nose and Mathias snorted. He could already feel sweat on the back of his neck. Even more irritating was the sweat on his wrists. He knew most people wouldn't think twice about it, but sweating around his wrists felt disgusting. He mentally shrugged and dug in deeper as he ran through the woods. Nathaniel was ahead of him by a few paces, but he didn't care because running full out was exhilarating. The ground was firm under his feet and he pushed against it and surged ahead of his friend. The two played tag for a few minutes, dodging in and out of the trees while increasing their speed. The hope was for one of them to miscalculate and run full tilt into the side of tree. Neither one succumbed to any bouts of clumsiness, this time, and the chase continued.

As he ran, he felt the stress of the day melt away. His mind churned with his mother's request. Mathias couldn't believe that she still didn't understand why he didn't speak to his brother. His friends were more like family than his blood. They had been the ones to keep him safe and encourage him to do more, instead of steal from him. Before he went down the memory path that could ruin his night out with his friends, he caught movement out of the side of his eye. Nathaniel had caught back up with him and with a haughty look, put on a burst of speed and nearly ran over the rabbit that dashed under his feet.

Mathias growled low in his throat and turned after the rabbit. His eyes narrowed as the dark form zagged away from him toward the tree line. He pushed against the moist earth and flattened his barrel shaped body closer to the ground. The rabbit gave him a good chase, move back and forth, trying hard to outrun him. The small creature gave him a workout and as his paws crunched against the rocks and sticks, he relaxed.

Until a dark shape cut in front of him. Mathias pushed harder, he knew if Nathaniel reached the rabbit this time, it would be over. It a desperate move, he pushed to the right and then dove to the left to catch the rabbit between his sharp teeth. One quick snap of its neck finished the job and he dropped it to the ground. Nathaniel came closer, making Mathias's hackles raise and growl form in the back of his throat. He picked up the rabbit and carried it back to the meeting circle, where the rest of the pack regrouped after their own runs. He dropped the rabbit in a pile of other kills and made his way back to his clothes.

His bones popped and elongated as he shifted out of his wolf form. After a few seconds, he stood as a man and pulled on his clothes. He stumbled as a warm hand clapped him hard on the back. He looked over his shoulder into Nathaniel's smiling face.

"I love the full moon, don't you? Our group runs are the shit."

Mathias gave a quick laugh and went to join his pack in celebration.

"And you wanted to waste it watching girls tumble around in gelatin," he reminded his friend.

"Hold on, why wasn't I told about this?"

Mathias turned to face their friend Travon, who approached them pulling a shirt over his head.

"Damn, knew I shoulda asked you first," Nathaniel grumbled. "Why didn't I?"

"Because it's a stupid idea," Mathias said. "Where's G?"

"Over with Marcus learning to be the next Alpha," Travon said. "He'll join us later. Come on, if we plan to eat, we've got some rabbits to clean."

Mathias held in a groan.

"What kind of werewolf acts like a damn wuss about skinning a rabbit?" Nathaniel mocked.

"The kind who is more used to being a man and not wolf," he snapped back.

He ignored the laughter from his friends and went to get the job done so he could enjoy the rest of the party.

Chapter 3

Two months later, Siona held tight to the case sitting on the seat next to her as the plane bumped down and stuttered along the runway. She looked around and noted no one else was panicking, so most likely they weren't crashing. She actually had no fear of flying, but she knew how delicate the balance of mirrors in here telescope were and cringed. It was doubtful that they would actually shift or move, but there was a possibility, since the plane moved about around two hundred miles per hour along a strip of asphalt as they landed. She relaxed as the plane slowed as it taxied into the gate.

I wonder why it is called taxiing to the gate. I'm sure it is some antiquated term or method for moving the plane or perhaps the layout of the airport. Okay were are here and the case looks to be in one solid piece. Now people can leave and quit throwing shade my way like I'm carrying a bomb or something. I almost wish they would have plied me with a million questions instead of sitting there with a silent curiosity growing into fear. Then again, they are probably just hangry; the cheap ole airlines could actually give us a proper snack. Like spending three dollars a person is going to make a dent in the billions of dollars quarterly these jerks bring in. Maybe I'm the hangry one.

She took a deep breath as they finally made it to the gate and sat back. Siona had never really enjoyed flying, the change in pressure and dehydrating atmosphere made it completely uncomfortable for her. It took almost ten minutes for the plane to empty. She also didn't understand those who rushed to stand, only to have to shuffle their way out of the plan. Siona had requested the very last row of seats for herself and her scope. This way no one would kick the back of their seats and jostle her equipment. She turned on her phone and texted her mother. She smiled at the overuse of emoji in the response and finally stood. She pulled her roller cart from overhead storage and then tried not to grunt as she lifted the 65 pound case onto it.

Siona made it quickly through the airport and into her mother's arms. She was rather amazed at how quickly she made it from plane to the baggage claim. She hugged her dad and then looked around.

"I forgot how small this airport is," she said.

"That's only because you're used to JFK, which should have its own zip code," her mother said. "We're not going to be at cousin Ella's after all. Aunt Sadie said we could stay with her, away from all the chaos. I think it's probably more likely that she wants more time with us. She still feels the need to look after me since Mama died. She was surprised you decided to stay in a hotel, so expect a few questions about that. Let's go get you settled before tonight's meet up."

"You just said a mouthful. Long drive?"

"Oh, yes," her father said.

Siona grabbed hold of her dolly and walked over to the belt to grab her suitcase. Her father interceded by grabbing the bag. She smiled as he raised an eyebrow in question about the dolly and she shook her head. He laughed at her possessiveness over her scope, but said nothing. She loved that her parents accepted the fact she would rather carry the heavy case instead of her clothes. She walked out the automatic doors and felt like someone had pressed her face into a steaming hot washcloth.

"You look surprised," her mother said. "It's this warm back home."

"I somehow expected it to be cooler here. I think it might be worse. Is it always like this?" she asked her mother, fanning herself. "Ninety-two degrees of welcoming heat. Hello, Michigan."

They got into the rental car and quickly made their way to her great-aunt's house. The lack of traffic was novel and Siona rubber-necked the whole way. Businesses and restaurants lined the main street they traveled on, but there were no sky scrapers. There were barely any two story buildings, and the grocery store stood in a lone building with a huge parking lot.

"This is so different from home," Siona murmured. "It looks pretty empty. Where is the city from here? Is it always so quiet?"

"Yes, I guess it's quiet. But this is very different from what I grew up with," her mother commented. "This is actually really built up."

Siona turned to stare at her mother and shrugged as her mother laughed at the expression covering her face.

"Seriously, there were a lot more undeveloped field and houses."

"I can't imagine that you acclimated to New York easily then," Siona said. "Didn't you feel like there was too much chaos?"

"Oh, there was plenty of chaos, but I had help."

"Yes, yes. I know that story all too well. Spare me the sappy details," Siona mock groaned.

The ride was over in twenty minutes and she exited the car, surprised.

"Wow, I thought you said Aunt Sadie lived fifteen miles from the airport," she said.

"Oh honey, everything is 20 minutes away when you're in Flint."

Siona followed her parents up to the door, but could have never prepared herself for the amount of people in the house. Granted she could have fit about four of her apartments into the square footage, but there were at least fifty people present.

"Si, come meet your great aunt Sadie," her mother said, leading her through the fray.

"Oh my, Crystal, she is beautiful," the older woman said, pulling Siona into a hug. "She looks just like Althea."

Siona accepted the warm hug from her great aunt and smiled.

"Good to meet you again, Aunt Sadie," she said.

"Lawd. Listen to this child's city accent," her aunt cackled. "For all that you look like your family; you sure don't sound like us. Then again, Chrissie, you sound more and more like you're from that place too."

"I've been there for thirty years, Auntie," her mother laughed. "You remember my husband, Charles?"

Siona stood quietly by her parents' side as they made the rounds through the house. There was no way she was going to remember all of the names that were given to her. She managed to sneak away and stood to one side, in a small hallway, while her mother and father talked animatedly with some cousins. There was so much laughing and jostling it took her a few moments to notice the two people who had joined her in the safe haven.

"Don't worry, despite all of us looking alike, you will learn who is who soon enough. I'm Kayla; your Great Aunt Louise was my grandmother. Kinetra is my mom."

Siona ran through who all the great aunts were: Sadie, Louise, Linda, Cheryl and Dorothea. There was her grandmother Althea and the sole male child, Keith, who was spoiled by his sisters.

"I'm Siona," she said with a smile.

"Of course you are. We've been hearing stories about you and your mom's arrival for days now. Plus you have that accent."

Kayla appeared to be about her age, but maybe stood five feet tall, petite against her own five foot nine. Siona wanted to laugh at how much of a family resemblance most of her kin did have. No doubt theirs were the stronger genetic sets. Kayla had the same shaped eyes—but hers were brown, and if her hair hadn't been pressed to fall straight down her back, probably would have looked just like Siona's own curls.

"This is Little Keith," Kayla said.

"Four minutes doesn't count," said the man who towered over both of them.

Siona looked at her other cousin who had an irritated glower on his face, which was nearly identical to his sister's.

"And still called *Little* because he is Great Uncle Keith's namesake,"

"Yeah, I go by Keith these days," he said. "I haven't been called little anything since I hit six feet three. So you are the famous cousin from New York?"

Siona laughed. "I'm famous?"

"Oh, sure. Well, if you listen to family rumors," Keith said. "You are the one who works at the famous planetarium. Uncle Keith just loves to brag on about you."

Siona was curious about the man who would brag about her, considering she hadn't seen him since she was fourteen years old.

"Well, I guess that is me. I work in research at the Hayden, but it is far from a glorious job. I do a lot of data mining and report writing."

"You are going to need to make it sound much more interesting when all these people ask you about it," Keith said. "How much longer, Kayla?"

The loud sigh and huge eye roll made Siona smile. She had been immediately comfortable with the two of them, and she hoped that she would be invited to hang out. The last thing she wanted to do was hang out with her parents, looking clingy and shy. Her cousins seemed to be easy going. She looked around the room and made eye contact with her mom, across the room. She gave a wink and smile which were returned. Her parents disappeared from view as they walked to the other side of the room.

"We have ten more minutes, before we can leave without too much backlash," Kayla said to Keith and then turned to face Siona. "I promised my mom that we would hang out at least an hour before leaving. We have a show in three weeks, so we have been spending as much time as possible getting ready. Keith is just itching to get back to it. He forgets it's easier being a boy in this family."

"Right, except they hate my business," Keith grunted and left them in the hallway as he went to grab snacks from the kitchen.

"Don't mind him. He already likes you," Kayla said with an infectious grin. "He really is focused on his work."
"I don't mind. I'm just glad to find family my age here," Siona said. "What kind of show?"
"Well, feel free to hang out with us," Kayla said. "We have an interview with some costume designers coming up at the local convention in a few weeks. Keith and I have our own small costume design studio, so he is stressing about getting everything done in time."

Siona couldn't help but turn to look at Keith and immediately felt embarrassed as her cousin laughed at her.

"He's straight."

Her cheeks blossomed into a full blush.

"I ...didn't... I mean... gosh. I am embarrassed," Siona muttered.

"It's the reaction he gets a lot," Kayla explained. "At least you did it while he wasn't here. Now you can act cool and calm when he mentions it to you. It will impress him."

"I don't care either way," she finally managed to stammer out. "Before I make it any worse, let me just say you two seem fun. I would be happy to hang out with you."

Siona tried to pull herself together as Keith walked back toward them with a plate full of food, wrapped and ready to go.

"You made a to-go plate?" Kayla scoffed. "Seriously, you're gonna be one of those people? Anyhow, let's go say good-bye so we can leave. We're taking Siona with us, so deal."

"We're going to make costumes," Keith said.

Siona nodded calmly at the challenge somehow offered in those words.

"Awesome, I look forward to seeing what you make."

She was proud of herself for keeping a neutral look on her face as she walked by him and into the living room again. She found her parents and smiled.

"I'm going to hang out with Kayla and Keith," she said to her mom.

"I'm glad. You should have some fun with kids your age. Call or text me after you get back to your hotel room."

Siona gave her a quick hug and walked through the room and to the kitchen, where she smothered a laugh at Kayla, who had also made a to-go plate of food. She was going to make a snarky

33

remark when a flier on the refrigerator caught her attention. She walked over and after reading it, grabbed the paper.

"Can you drop me off here?" she asked and hastily added. "After, I come see the costumes and everything you are working on? It looks like tonight if the only time they will be running this event while I am here."

"I'm pretty sure if I said 'no', you would crumple," Kayla teased. "You should see your face right now."

"I'm from New York, I am tougher than that," Siona scoffed, rolling her eyes. "But, yes, I would walk there if I had to."

"Fine, we'll drop you off. It doesn't start for a few hours, so we have plenty of time. Keith, let's go."

It took them almost ten minutes to wade through the spillover of family that conversed in the back yard. When they got through the small crowd, the made their way to the street. Kayla walked to a maroon Chevy Impala and smiled with pride.

"It took me four years, and a lot of costume sales, but this baby is mine free and clear," she said with a smile.

The mention of the car kicked Siona's brain into high gear.

"Oh, wait. I need to go get my case."

She walked through the yard and over to the street where their rental car was parked. She grabbed the case from the trunk and made her way out to where her cousins waited. Smiling at Kayla, who popped the trunk for her, Siona carefully stowed it away and hopped in the back seat. She had planned to set it up in the backyard, but the party would be a better place.

The chatter was idle and covered various topics over the short ten minute ride. They pulled up to a small strip mall off a main road that was completely dark, minus a few parking lot lights. Keith opened the door and flipped on the lights. Siona felt her mouth drop as she walked into their shop. When Kayla had mentioned costumes, she had imagined fairy dresses for little girls or pirate ensembles for little boys. What was before her, were far more elaborate and clearly works of art. The detail and precision of each outfit and the accompanying accoutrement showed the many hours of work going into each costume.

"This is my creation for my Kingdom of Talinwan elemental elf princess. It took me about three months to make, including all of the electronic work," Kayla said, showing off a piece with pride.

Siona had no idea what the Kingdom of Talinwan was, but the finished costume featured ornate leather-and-metal armor, as well as two thin rapiers and a shield.

"That is really impressive," she said. "I've never heard of the Kingdom of Talinwan."

Keith chuckled deeply. "That was pretty evident by the look on your face. One of my friends here created the game. So far it's a local game, but with the show in a few weeks, he is hoping to debut it for the bigger companies. It's your standard RPG, but Kayla and I were brought in early to design the costume looks for each kind of character."

Kayla held out a costume for Siona to inspect while her brother talked.

"The props are the best part."

Her eyebrows rose at her cousin, as she hefted a sword and with a push of a button, it illuminated from inside giving the illusion of being covered in flames.

"It took almost two years to get it right, but it's worth it in the end. Keith does all the costume design, but I add all the cool parts. We're just hoping to get noticed by a wider audience. Make yourself at home; we've got some things to finish."

Siona continued to look around for a while, as her cousins got to work. After an hour, she nudged Kayla.

"It's time. Do you mind dropping me off?"

"Here, just take my keys and don't crash my car," Kayla said, distracted by her leather awl. "Turn left out of the driveway and left on Crapo and right onto Kearsley. You can't miss it."

"Okay, I'll just put it into my GPS and find it. You sure about the car?"

"Yes. After watching you baby that case, I know you will be careful. Give me a second and I'll text you my number in case you get lost."

A few moments later Siona drove toward her first Star Party in Michigan with a huge grin plastered all over her face.

Chapter 4

Matthias smiled as he put the finishing touches on his weekly report. Tonight was the last night of "Star Party: The Dog Days of Summer". He grinned wide at the sign. The title had been hard won. He started off with Star Party: After Dark, and when he shared it with Nathaniel the non-stop laughter convinced him that he might want to change the title. He did owe a lot to his friend though. Star Parties usually took a hiatus during the summer, the later sunset meant a smaller crowd and was harder to justify. Nathaniel had been the one to suggest making the party for the aficionados who would stay up later to experience the summer skies. One small grant from a private corporation later, and the new venture was a go. Mathias had hit up all his pack mates to help spread the word and fliers all over Genesee County. He was hoping for a decent turn out. Attendance for June and July had been remarkable and he hoped to go out with strong numbers.

"Mathias, I was wondering if you could help me."

The soft voice caught his attention as he walked out of the planetarium, across the parking lot and to the small field in front of the dome that housed the gatherings. Mr. Hershel was his most devoted party goer, but at eighty-six, often needed some help setting up the equipment. He also needed more human interaction. Most of his friends weren't as spry, or as interested in the stars, and his family lived down in Cincinnati. Mathias smiled and walked over to help the man set up. At nine o'clock it was just getting dark, so it left him plenty of time to help out the older man and still get his small lecture ready to go. Most others party goers milled about as they arranged their own scopes.

A half hour later, he was pleased not only with having Mr. Hershel all set up, but the attention of the twenty other people who had decided to show. In addition to the few regulars, there were a lot of new faces, and a few even had brought their kids. Thankfully they were well behaved and showed a genuine interest in the sky as well. The chatter was low and general as the group set up in the warm weather to explore the summer sky. Mathias was just finishing his lecture to the group as they tracked Mars as it passed in front of the Beehive cluster, when a maroon Chevy Impala drove into the parking lot. He forced himself to continue the conversation, instead of stopping midsentence to stare as the newcomer exited the car.

She was tall but slender; he figured around his height at five ten, with her spiral curled hair pulled up into a low bun against her neck. Her sundress was a purple tie-dyed pattern and fell just below her knees. His interest tripled as he watched her lug a 2x2 case out of the trunk of the car. As she swayed back, it was evident the case was heavy. Mathias wanted to offer his help, but as soon as it cleared the trunk, she easily carried it over to a section of the lawn and set it down. He watched in rapt attention as she quickly and efficiently set up, at the outer perimeter of the group.

"Mathias, who is the young lady?"

"I'm not sure, Mr. Hershel. She is new, but clearly knows what she is doing."

"That is a big telescope," Mr. Hershel observed.

"That is a Dobsian, the Cadillac of scopes," he replied. "I've been eyeing that one for a while. It's amazing."

"The girl is pretty amazing too. Just beautiful."

"Yes," Mathias said.

He deliberately kept the answer short. Mr. Hershel might be eighty-six but as the elder explained it, he had some seventy decades to perfect his game. One that often include putting the smack down on the younger competition. Mathias grinned because the older man definitely had some tricks up his sleeve and it was fun to watch him work.

"Excuse me."
Mathias looked up into wide hazel eyes, and swallowed hard. Her face was diamond shaped with eyes and nose in perfect alignment. She also had freckles scattered across her nose and cheeks.

"Oh no, Miss, excuse us for being so rude. How can we help you?"

Mathias was jolted back into interaction as Mr. Hershel made a move, which should have been his.

"I need the latitude and longitude of our location," she said. "Or the zip code, if you don't have those coordinates."

"Oh darlin' that would be 43.0100° N, 83.6900° W. I'm no novice to the stars, but apparently neither are you," Mr. Hershel said with a smile. "Will you give me a tour of that lovely Dobsian scope you have? I've been lusting after such a fine thing for a while."

Mathias shook his head as the older man offered up his arm, and the young lady accepted. Not only had Mr. Hershel stepped in, but he used the information Mathias had given him earlier to set up his telescope to make his play. He knew he would definitely have to step up his game if he planned to get her attention. He amended his first thought about it being fun to watch the older man flirt. With the little display Mr. Hershel had just made, he knew it would be a serious challenge to gain the attention of their new-comer. He stayed closer enough to hear the conversation.

"I'm Leroy Hershel, what is your name?"

"Siona Carter."
"Oh, you from the Carter family down on Hempfield?"

"My great aunt Sadie lives over there," she exclaimed. "I'm here visiting for a family reunion."
"I know Sadie well; we go to the same church…"

Mathias stared in disbelief as Mr. Hershel got information from their guest. He double checked to make sure his mouth wasn't hanging open, as he learned about her. He figured this was his good karma coming back to him. Mr. Hershel tended to work his nerves just a bit during the star parties, but tonight he made up for every irritation he had ever caused Mathias. He watched the older man peer through the eyepiece of the scope. Siona leaned close and then stood up and tapped a tablet held in her hand. That was all he got to watch before other group members took his attention.

Forty minutes later everyone chatted and enjoyed the view of the night sky. Mathias actually preferred the summer time parties. It was quieter and darker because most businesses were closed and didn't spill their light into the sky, meaning much less city burn to contend with. The only regret he had was not following his gut and taking the group to view stars at remote locations.

"Okay, I am going to talk about the eight inch Celestion, the new grant got us. If you want to come over, I am going to show you how to set up the German Equatorial mount and then walk you through how to use this reflector scope."

Mathias launched into his small prepared lecture about the scope. While he loved space, giving lectures wasn't his most favorite thing to do. Though he would never admit it to anyone, it still made him nervous to speak in front of a group of people. He made sure to pace himself and breathe at regular intervals. After the speech he invited people up to look through the scope and explore. As he walked around, helping other set their scopes to find a particular star or cluster he overheard Mr. Hershel talking again to Siona.

"It's so bright, it never looks like that in my telescope," the older man remarked.

"It's all about the size, the bigger the lens and mirror, the more light you can collect, the further you can see," she said while looking at her tablet. She seemed to have an idea and looked at her watch then back at the tablet. "In fact you can also see really small objects that are very close too. Want to see something really cool?"

Mathis walked closer as Siona began adjusting the controls; the machine came to life and hummed smoothly as the motorized mount panned the instrument across the night sky until locking onto something. He watched her peer through the eyepiece and then look back at Mr. Hershel with a soft smile.

"Come look."

Mr. Hershel looked through the eyepiece and then actually gasped "Is that the space station?"

After a few seconds, no one was at their telescopes. All the equipment sat abandoned as the entire group now clustered around Siona. Mathias found himself shuffled toward the back of the group.

"Ok just take a quick peek then let someone else look, we only have 3 minutes before it's out of view" she cautioned the group members while looking at all of the rest the anxious sky watchers.

Mathias was fairly sure he could have set himself on fire while juggling chainsaws and still not peel them away. But he wasn't jealous; he was impressed, he had never seen the group this engaged. Siona was not only good and instructing the crowd, but she was having a great time with it. He stood watching with a smile, when her eyes turned to him.

41

"Do you want a look?"

"Please," he said.

Mathias leaned over and looked through the scope and at the space station. He spent a quick moment looking, before backing up and looking over her scope. The mirrors perfectly aligned and it was obviously well cared for.

"Nice scope," he said.

"Thanks, it was my graduation gift," she said with a smile. "I think my parents have finally gotten over the shock that I turned down a new car and asked for this instead."

"I can imagine," he said with a chuckle. "Although I have to say, this is the best graduation gift I have ever seen."

"Thanks. This is an amazing event. I'm glad I came."

"They don't have star parties where you are from?"

"Oh they do; we view from the High Line Park. We even have solar observation parties in Central Park, but it's awesome to come to a new state and see a different section of the sky."

"So, you came all the way to Michigan for my star party?" he teased.

He watched her process the information and smiled proudly. Her eyes narrowed and she tilted her head a bit. The quirk of her lips, made him wonder what she had wanted to say.

"I'm here for a family reunion, but when family got to be a bit much for me, I headed out here," she said. "Your party, huh? You're like a manager or something?"

""Yea, I run the programs here at the Longway," he said.

Mathias waited for her to be impressed and maybe even ask for a tour. He smiled at how smoothly he had interjected that it was his gig into their conversation. Then he saw her lips twitch again. He had the feeling he was either being set up to be the butt

42

of a joke, or even worse, she was laughing at him and he had no idea why.

"Oh, it's such a cute little planetarium," Siona said.

"It's the largest one in Michigan," he offered.

"Ahhh," she said and then redirected her gaze into her scope lens as her tablet beeped.

He watched her alternate between looking through the scope and making notes on her tablet, and tried again to make conversation.

"Is the party here like the ones in New York?"

"Pretty much, a group of people gathering around, talking about stars. Although we do get some pretty interesting lecturers to come out and talk with our group," she said. "This is a fun group though, more interest and less competition."

He started to wrack his brain for something to say that wouldn't result in her wanting to laugh at him and almost breathed a sigh of relief as Mr. Hershel came toward them.

"Mathias, I need your help to get the Celestion set up," the elder man said. "Oh unless you would like to do the honors, Siona. That is one fine scope there."

"No thank you, Mr. Hershel. I am sure your program director wants to keep his hands on his new toy."

"Well then darlin', perhaps while he sets it all up for me, you can show me more about your beautiful piece."

Mathias shook his head and walked back over to where the new and shiny, but ultimately ignored, piece of equipment sat. Siona had stolen the night by showing the group the space station. He looked up into the dark night sky and sighed. He never got tired of the amazing view. Of course it helped that he got to run under the full moon each month, but the stars amazed him more. He was still working with the equipment when Mr. Hershel came back to him.

"You gonna ask that girl out?"

"Excuse me?"

"Look son, I've known you for a few years now and you haven't dated anyone more than a few times," Mr. Hershel said. "Siona is only here for a few weeks, so it should be enough time for you to have some fun with a beautiful woman. She will leave to go home and you won't feel compelled to offer a commitment that makes you feel trapped."

"I don't know if that fraternizing with party goers is a good idea, he said. "And I have never felt trapped."

Up until that moment Mathias had thought throwing the side eye was a young person trait. Mr. Herschel, however, apparently had spent eighty-six years perfecting the right amount of shade into his look.

"At least three young women you have mentioned were only talked about up until that first date. Then you never talked about them again."

"I don't recall talking about my dates during star parties," Mathias shrugged.

"You didn't, but you do talk at work to your co-workers. And for those of us who are around to see the shows, we hear things too," Mr. Hershel said. "Just ask her out. I'm sure you will have a great time."

Mathias started to shake his head and say something. For as wise as Mr. Hershel had always been about offering advice, he was dead wrong about Mathias's dating life. Though the short term dating idea was appealing, especially since the full moon had just passed and Siona would be long gone before the next one came around.

"I set it all up for you. She has never had a Coney dog," Mr. Herschel said, interrupting his thoughts.

"What? How could she live near the original Coney Island and never had had a Coney dog?" Mathias asked.

"Because they originated in Michigan? Sounds like the perfect conversation starter when you ask her out," Mr. Hershel said. "Do make her aware that the Flint style is much better than that goopy—tomato based —no bean having— chili style Detroit Coney."

The disdain caught him off guard and Mathias laughed deeply.

"Thank you. Once I get things shut down for the night, I'll talk to her. And *if* I ask her out, I will make sure she only eats the Flint style Coney dog."

Mathias went back to enjoying the star party. He shook his head with a wry smile. The old man was full of surprises that night, but he did give Mathias an opening to find out more about Siona. As eleven o'clock came, he began to pack up the telescopes and take them into the planetarium. He moved quickly, realizing the old man was right and he should try to have some fun during his two weeks of vacation.

Chapter 5

Siona retrieved her case from nearby and got ready to break down her telescope. She smiled to herself, happy with how the night had gone. Her phone chimed and she looked down to find a text from Kayla letting her know that she and Keith would be pulling an all-nighter at their shop. She also got instructions to pick them up at nine the next morning. She sent a quick reply back and turned back to her scope. She twisted the clamps and began to remove the eyepiece.

New York never got as dark as where she currently stood and it was amazing what else she could see in the skies. Not to mention the difference being in another state offered. She began to play with the idea of borrowing the rental car and visiting some of the other planetariums in Michigan.

"Thanks for letting me see the space station."

The small soft voice belonged to a serious looking little girl standing a few feet away from Siona. She guessed the child was around eight years old. She was tiny with blonde hair and brown eyes. She reminded Siona of some of the children from the school programs at the Hayden. Granted she never worked with them, but she did pass a lot of them on her way home.

"My pleasure," she said. "I'm Siona, what's your name?"

"Katie."

"Well Katie, I'm glad you enjoyed it. We had the luck of clear skies tonight. Do you come to these star parties often?"

"Oh, yes. My parents are in the Genesee Astronomical Society. We meet here every month. Can you tell me more about your telescope? I've never seen one like it."

Siona slowly began to put her equipment away, but kept up a steady stream of chatter explaining the parts and how they all came together to create the images. The girl seemed truly interested and often asked questions. Katie followed her as she walked back to the car and opened the trunk. As she put the case back in the car, she had an idea. She popped the case back open and after making sure she could make it happen, turned back to the girl.

"Do you want to build your own telescope?" she asked.

Siona had never seen eyes widen so far, nor a smile so bright. She pulled out the needed items from the side storage folders of the case.

"Seriously?"

"Absolutely. Here, you can help me."

She handed the girl a few pieces of thick black paper, two magnifying glasses and black tape. Siona had to take almost everything out of the telescope case before she found the bonding glue. She closed the case and trunk and smiled down at the child.

"Let's go over to that picnic table and make your scope.

Katie skipped ahead of her and had set the pieces down on the table.

"Okay, I'm going to break these two magnifying glasses so we can use the lenses. This large one has three times magnifying power and this small one has six."

"Are you sure you want to break them? I don't want you to wreck your stuff," Katie said.

"Really, it's okay. I'm explaining how to do this, so you can make your own someday," Siona said. "Not to mention, it makes a loud cracking sound and I didn't want to scare you."

As predicted, cracking the plastic lens cases was nice and loud. Siona carefully explained what she did step by step; noticing the little girl's serious engagement. She was thankful the magnifying glass frames broke away easily. Far too many times she had cracked a lens trying to take it out.

"Now, Katie. I want you to roll this piece of the black paper around the large lens. It does have sticky glue on it, so you need to be very careful. Do you think you can do that?"

Katie nodded eagerly, but took the task seriously as she rolled the lens on to the paper until it made a tube. Siona helped her tape it closed, and then let the girl repeat her task with the smaller lens. The small tube easily fit inside the larger one. Siona pulled them apart and taped around the center and handed the small scope back to the girl.

"Take a look. The images that are close up will be inverted. The nice thing is that in astronomy it doesn't matter whether the planet is upside down or not," Siona grinned. "And the really cool thing? This same design was used by Galileo."

She watched Katie, gently take the homemade scope and point it towards the skies. She smiled as the girl made appreciative squeals, as she spun around looking up. Siona cleaned up the broken plastic and tossed it into a nearby bin. She almost tripped over the little girl when she turned back around and found her standing there.

"Thank you."

She was caught off guard Katie threw herself into her arms. "This is the best present I have ever gotten."

"You are very welcome," she said.

She gave the girl a firm hug and then waved as the girl ran back to her parents. Siona shook her head, pleased at how the night had gone.

"I think you just stole my most ardent admirer," a rich voice said behind her.

She turned around to meet a set of mesmerizing butterscotch colored eyes. They wrinkled at the corner as the smile covered his face, not that she exactly was staring at him. More that she noticed how his high cheekbones were covered with light stubble, and he had a well-shaped mouth. Siona silently chided herself for even thinking of the words "well-shaped", and gave herself a mental snap back into place.

"Now you know the trick; show your admirers how to make a telescope," she as laughter bubbled up.

He joined her in laughter and held out his hand.

"I'm Mathias, I forgot to introduce myself earlier," he said.

She nodded; she had heard Mr. Herschel call his name. She was surprised she hadn't noticed his eyes earlier. Given they were making it hard for her to concentrate.

"Siona," she said. "Don't worry about your fans leaving; I'm only here for a few weeks. You can take the number one spot again at the next party."

"Well, Siona. How about I treat you to a Flint style Coney dog to celebrate your first star party in Michigan?"

She felt her eyes widen a bit. While she expected more banter about the telescopes or maybe even about her stealing his program from him that night, she never imagined he would be asking her out.

"I'm going to guess there is more than one style," she ventured.

"Not if you're from Flint," he said with a smile.

For a heartbeat, Siona waffled. She really didn't know him. He could be some murderous cad, who would kidnap her and leave her body parts for her grief stricken parents to find. Or, alternatively, he could be a nice guy, who also liked stars, who wanted to take her on an impromptu date her first night in town. Nothing exciting was waiting for her back at her hotel. She would just have to text Kayla and let her know what was going on, as a backup plan.

"Sure, that sounds like fun," she said. "Let me get my telescope secured properly and I need to text my cousin. I have her car."

"Great. I am going to put away the equipment and will meet you back out here in about ten minutes," he said.

Siona secured the case in the trunk in record time. The rest of the time waiting for him was spent in a flurry of text messages to and from her cousin. She promised to text the name of the diner, refused to take a covert picture, and agreed to answer a phone call in thirty minutes. She wanted to laugh at how being in Michigan completely flipped her life around. All in four hours. She grinned into the darkness. If Tony in HR could only see her now… She could only imagine the kind of bets she had just won for him.

She didn't date much in New York. It wasn't because she worked third shift. In the city that never slept, plenty of people worked third shift. Siona just found that the guys who were good to talk about astrophysics, wanted to hear themselves talk about it. Women in her field were far and few between, so the men were allowed to think she didn't know very much. Especially since she had decided to take a few years off before going after her graduate degree. The other problem was the men who weren't scientists. Once they asked what she did, and she had the chance to talk about her work, she found many of them too intimidated for a second date.

She hoped Mathias wouldn't cringe to learn she worked at the Hayden.

"Good job, dummy," she muttered to herself. "You already went and called his dome a cute little thing. Here's the plan: tone down the snobbery, have a Coney dog and enjoy a guy who likes the stars too."

She cut off the one-sided conversation as she saw him walking across the lot toward her.

"Got your escape plan all set?" he asked in a teasing tone.

"Wow. You throw it out there just like that?" she asked with a laugh. "Will I need one? Should I invite Mr. Herschel as backup?"

"Not at all. I'm going to show you the best Coney dog place around here, and talk to you about the stars," he said. "But since I am still kind of a stranger, I'm sure your cousin will call you in about twenty minutes to see if you need rescuing."

Her laugh deepened. "Thirty actually, and I had to promise to follow you and then text her the address."

She was glad when he joined the laughter.

"Good plan. You never can be too safe," he said. "Although, I'm pretty sure Mr. Herschel would hunt me down, if something happened to you. He knows your family and he likes you, a lot."

"Funny, he said the same thing about you," she said.

Siona got the instant gratification of seeing heat cover his face. Rarely had she been able to make a guy blush in casual fun. Not to mention, he was damn cute looking embarrassed. She was impressed at how quickly he recovered as he gave her the address. She passed it on to Kayla, who assured her it was a good place, and to be sure to try the chili fries. The trip was about ten minutes and she shook her head. Her mother wasn't kidding, everything was close. The restaurant was brightly lit and pretty full, but they found an empty corner booth and took it.

"My cousin said the chili fries were amazing," she said. "But I like my fries plain. Okay let's try these hot dogs of yours. You're gonna have to order, since I don't know what should or shouldn't be on them."

Siona waited until Mathias was done ordering to ask the waitress for mayonnaise and hot sauce.

"Where in New York are you from?" he asked.

"Manhattan," she said, pleased that he had paid attention before. "How about you? Are you from Burton?"
"Nope. Flint boy, born and raised," he said with a smile. "Are your folks from Burton?"

She nodded, not sure what kind of question and answer session they would have. In fact, she had called it a date in her mind, but a slight flutter of panic began, as she realized he might not consider this anything more than a friendly chat. Although, she recalled his comment about her escape call, and those only usually happened on dates, or so she thought.

"My mom grew up here, but moved to New York for grad school, met my dad and decided to stay," Siona said.

She sighed in relief because their food came out because she was starving. The hotdogs were covered in some kind of meat sauce that smelled great. After getting her mayonnaise and hot sauce, she carefully mixed it into a dip for her fries. She noticed the amused smile on his Mathias's lips.

"Welcome to Michigan and your first Coney dog," he said.

"Thank you."

Siona picked up the hotdog and took a healthy bite. She chewed carefully and nodded her head.

"This is pretty good," she said. "Although, why put meat on the top of the hotdog? I mean, it's already a meat product."

"I really don't know," Mathias said with a shrug. "But it's tasty. What is your concoction?"

Siona pushed it toward him.

"Try it. It's not too hot."

She watched him taste it and try to like it.

"I'm sure it would be great, if I liked mayonnaise."

She deliberately widened her eyes.

"Don't tell me you are one of those sandwich spread people," she said in mock horror.

A laugh escaped when he matched her exaggerated expression.

"Oh, good god, no. I don't like either of them. The texture is just wrong," he said. "Don't get me started about pudding or jello."

"So what do you like on your fries?"

"Pepper. If I want to get really fancy, some mustard," Mathias said and after a drink asked. "What got you interested in the stars?"

"I just always have been. One of my most favorite memories is when I was about five. My parents had taken me to the planetarium to see a show. After it was over, I went over to the control station, and the amazing guy sitting there let me turn on and off different effects. He explained the controls and once I made the planets zoom in and out I was hooked," she said.

Her phone rang loudly and the diner went silent as "Twinkle, twinkle, little star," played. Siona felt her face heat as a blush covered it and she scrambled to answer the phone, amid the chuckles. At almost midnight there were a fair number of people, and she had caught their attention.

"Hey, Kayla," she said softly. "It's all good. I'll call you when I get back to my hotel. Talk to you later."

She tucked her phone back into her purse. When she looked up and across the table, Mathias was staring at her. While she wanted to gaze into his eyes, she instead cleared her throat.

"What about you?" she deflected. "How did you get interested in the skies?"

"My Pops was the janitor at the Longway for forty years. He took me there whenever I asked. Not only did I go often, but the head astronomer answered all of my questions and then some. I worked there all through high school and college. When Richard decided to retire, I was a year away from completing my master's degree. I was lucky enough to get hired as the director of educational programs," he said.

Siona's heart melted just a bit at his story. There was a slight pause as they ate their food. She finished before him, realizing that it was her first meal since earlier in the day. She hadn't eaten at the family gathering, and unlike her cousins, making a to-go plate wasn't her style. Although, she was seriously reconsidering the practice.

"Now that you know what I do," he said. "What do you do for a living?"

Siona met his eyes and swallowed a nervous giggle. She didn't want to sound like she was bragging, but she loved her job. She promised herself she'd talk about it for fifteen minutes tops.

Chapter 6

Mathias waited for the answer to his question a bit longer than he had expected. He continued to eat, while he watched her try to cover a smile and fail. Her giggle made him wonder if he had asked a sensitive question. She carefully placed her silverware across her plate, and then leaned back in the seat a bit. He couldn't understand why she would drag out her answer.

"I'm an astrophysicist," she said. "I work in research and development."

He watched he wait for a reaction, and raise an eyebrow at him. His brain spun as snippets of conversations clicked into lace. It grabbed onto the title she tossed out, and impressed him. While his own degree was in Astronomy, his masters was in education. He should have recognized a kindred soul when she lugged the big telescope out of the car trunk.

"At NYU?" he asked. "I hear they have a great program."

"They really do, I graduated from the program almost two years ago. At some point my plan is to go back and finish a graduate program, but I haven't started looking into them just yet. I wanted a break from studying and figured that spending time in the field would give me a better idea of what I want to research for my thesis."

Mathias felt his heart speed up just a bit as her face glowed as she talked about her plans. He was glad that she didn't come out and announce that she was a professor. Although she had certainly seemed like she was a natural when instructing Katie on how to build a scope. He smiled at her as she elaborated on her answer.

"I do R&D with data from The Dish for the Hayden planetarium," she said nonchalantly. "Sometimes people are curious about what I am finding. Other times they just argue that my theories are wrong. Even better, because I happen to have my reproductive organs on the inside, I can't possibly begin to understand why I am so wrong. And then the condescending education begins."

I'm impressed she works at the Hayden; I bet she's first assistant to Dr. de Grasse Tyson. Wow, she is seriously into the research. Do I ask her what she is researching or will that lead me into the territory of maybe disagreeing with her and then we argue? That would be a terrible way to end a date. Oh crap, I said date. I don't need to complicate this.

Mathias kept the smile pasted on his face. Of course she worked at one of the top planetariums in the world. Not that he was embarrassed by the Longway, his planetarium was amazing. And quite frankly, it might not be as big as the Hayden, but with all of the updates it could stand toe to toe. It actually had the newest projection systems and had attracted program managers from all over the United States to preview how it worked. His internal pep talk restored him. How many times in his life would he find a beautiful woman who was just as interested in the skies as he was?

"What kind of research?"

"I work with data from the Cassini- Huygens Saturn expedition. Well the Huygens data from Titan. It's a lot of data mining and number crunching," she said. "Quite frankly, your job seems more exciting. You get to work with a whole group of people who are interested in the skies, and still find it fun. Making that telescope with Katie was the most fun I've had in a long while. I always have my head up in the stars, but sometimes it's nice to see that other people are still excited about the stars too."

He nodded; he was amazed when she so casually mentioned her work with the Dish. He loved his job and wouldn't change it for anything, but he was curious about the outcomes she would find. Mathias was drawn in when she talked about working with the little girl; her nose wrinkled and he again noticed the freckles on the tops of her cheeks. He realized being out with her, was the first outing with a woman where he was interested and engaged.

"I agree. I love being able to bring new programs to the kids. The excitement from them is amazing," he said.

"Do you design all of the programs?" she asked.

"Actually, I collaborate with the education department, but events like these parties are my baby. We have a full run of programs for kids to keep them interested the skies," he said.

"What kind of programs? Sadly, I have to admit- I rarely get to that area of our planetarium," she said. "Kids aren't really my thing."

"Seriously? What you did with Katie was amazing and you were a natural. The last program I led was making rockets," he grinned. "It was a huge program, and they stuck me with all the boys. I had twenty little rascals waiting to blow things up."

He spent the next twenty minutes, telling her about all the misadventures during the class. Mathias went into storytelling mode and in great detail entertained her with things exploding early, how baking soda ended up in almost every crevice of each boy there, and victory cheers and dances as their rockets launched. After their laughter died down over the many antics, there was a lull while he finished his food. He had done most the talking while she ate, so he tried to eat without looking like he was bolting his food. Mathias wasn't ready to part with her company just yet. He shoved the term 'date' away and decided to just enjoy their evening. He flagged down the waitress and ordered some pie for both of them. She smiled at him and ordered ice cream to go with hers. He was glad to have a woman who had no problem eating. The last date he had been on had all but refused to eat anything more than a side salad. He returned Siona's smile.

"So, your cousin was all good with your check in? Granted I'm no pro, but it seemed really quick. She's still good to leave you alone with me?" he asked. "Cute ring tone, by the way."

He enjoyed watching pink tinge her cheeks again. For a quick second, he realized he was enjoying every moment with her. It had been a while since he had been on a date — as Mr. Herschel had reminded him, but he couldn't remember any other date being so good. Similar backgrounds aside, Siona wasn't like any other woman he had met. She was self-assured and strong, but then would blush… and he would fall just a bit more. The pie arrived and Mathias watched as she ate half of her slice before looking back up at him.

"Yes, the check in was fine. Kayla was really excited to tell me they just had a last minute order called in, and only had two weeks to finish it. She and my cousin Keith are all excited about some upcoming show. Apparently some big name design person will be there," Siona said. "And what other kind of ringtone is a stargazer supposed to have?"

Mathias bit back a smile as she rapidly switched topics. While she wasn't particularly defensive, the tilt of her chin dared him to mock her about it. He had no intention of making her feel bad. He wanted her to hang out a while longer.

"I have Holst," he said with a dismissive shrug. "That is, when my roommate doesn't highjack my phone and put embarrassing ring tones on it."

He was happy to have thrown himself under the bus, when her eyes lit up. He knew he would have to be careful around her. She definitely had a mischievous sparkle going on. He was being sucked in fast, and once he thought about it – decided he didn't care.

"Like what?"

"Some hellacious thing called *the laughing baby rap*. I will spare you the horror of actually having to hear that thing, but imagine forty seconds of some baby laughing and cooing, set to a beat track. I think it was supposed to be cute, but it's the creepiest damn thing I have ever heard. And because the Universe has a sense of humor, it rang during a staff meeting," Matthias said. "The good news is that it was just me and my boss, and he found it amusing."

He shook his head at the memory. Needless to say, he showed Nathaniel his displeasure about the ring tone during their next run. They finished their desert while he grasped at straws on what further conversations to have. She didn't seem to be in any particular hurry, so he tried to find out more about her.

"I know you're here for a family reunion. How long are you staying?"

"Three weeks," she said. "My job forced me into it, because they are evil like that."

"They make you take vacation? How terrible and heavy handed of them to make sure you have time off."

He gave the best shocked face he could, and then waited a few seconds for an elaboration, but got none. He met her eyes and realized she was playing with him.

"Do I get the sordid details?"

"My lovely Human Resources department, being the nosy people they are, apparently have noticed a trend amongst researchers. Namely that we don't take a lot of vacation," she said.

"So they forced you to take one? Those horrible people working to ensure your health."

"They are much worse than that," Siona said.

Mathias didn't dare chuckle at the side eye she gave him. Even though he made no sound, his body language betrayed his mirth. After taking a few seconds to compose himself, he met her gaze and held it until she relented.

"They place bets on when we will take vacation. And when they learned I had a family reunion, not only did the head of HR grant my vacation time, she extended it by a week for me."

He gave into the chuckles then.

"No, I am not laughing at you," he said, holding up his hands in defense. "I am also on a forced vacation. Since the construction and grand reopening were huge events, I was told I would be taking a vacation. However, I delayed it by getting a grant to have the summer star parties."
"Oh, you don't normally don't do these in the summer?"

"It's usually too late at night to gather a crowd, so it's last on the list for funding," he said. "I am hoping that the decent turn outs will convince them otherwise."

Their bill arrived and Mathias slid it toward him. He winked at her.

"You couldn't possibly think that I would invite you out and make you pay for your first ever Coney dog?" he chided her gently. "Welcome to Flint."

"Thank you, Mathias."

The way his name rolled off her tongue made him want to kiss her. Although to be honest, he had wanted to kiss her from the moment she walked into his party. His brain churned and spun as he tried to figure out what else there was to do. He had no urge to share her attention, so the club was out. Maybe he could use their passion to his advantage.

"Are you up for a little more star gazing? I can't imagine you got any good viewing time behind the scope due to finding the space station and all," he said. "I know the perfect place, if you're not exhausted."

"Sure," she said excitedly. "I work third shift, so this is about half way through my night. I was kind of dreading going back to my hotel room and staring at the walls."

"Let me send a quick text and see if I can set this up," he said.

Mathias then sent the one string of words, he never thought he would have to use. *The monkey is hungry.* The emergency, woman-related, code had been created in high school. It had various meanings – sometimes it was a call for help, sometimes it was a heads up that privacy was needed and on nights like tonight, it meant a favor was needed. He prayed Gregory was somewhat awake and not occupied with his own woman.

A quick return text made sure it was him and not Nathaniel stealing the phone. Mathias sent a short text asking him to meet them at For-Mar's main gate, so they could have some premium sky. The text came back quickly and he sighed. Of course the condition was to tell all later, and Mathias had no choice but to agree.

"Okay, we are all good to go, now that my friend agreed to let us in. My idea of excitement has nothing to do with being arrested for trespassing," he said. "Do you want to carpool or drive separate? I know your cousin has rules."

"How far away is it?" she asked.

"About fifteen minutes, maybe twenty," he said and couldn't understand why she burst into giggles.

"I'll drive," she said.

Matthias gave her the address and promised to drive slowly. He kept careful watch in the rearview mirror to make sure she didn't get lost. As they turned off the main road, he realized that he missed spending the night at For-Mar watching the skies in peace.

He hadn't done it since his grad school insomnia nights. The park didn't have a front gate, but it was closely monitored. Gregory being aware of their presence meant no disturbances. He drove the winding path and finally stopped in the empty parking lot. There were a few picnic tables to the side and he sat down. He looked up into a perfectly clear sky and sighed. Siona soon joined him.

"This is beautiful," she said as she got out of the car. "I can't believe you don't camp out here to look into the skies every night."

"Before the upgrades to the dome, I used to spend a lot more time here. I should probably get back into the habit because I am just now realizing what I have missed."

He helped her unload her case, despite a side long glance from her. Mathias stood by as she set up her telescope. It was easy to tell she used her equipment often. Once it was done, she leaned over and peered through the eyepiece. The sigh of contentment hit him in the gut.

"Do you want a look?" she asked.

"Take your time. I live here, so I can see these skies any time I want."

Mathias smiled when she looked back at him over her shoulder. He longed to tell her that he had the best view anyhow, but didn't want to sound like a creep. He sat on the picnic table and smiled, he couldn't believe how great it was going.

Chapter 7

Siona woke as her phone buzzed again, a string of texts from her mother, reminded her about the day's activities. She acknowledged the schedule and asked for twenty minutes to get ready. She was certain it would take her weeks to get her schedule straightened out once she got home, but considering the night before, she had no complaints. A smile crossed her lips. After spending two hours at the park, she noticed that Mathias worked hard to conceal his yawns. He apologized profusely until she leaned in and kissed him.

Siona touched her lips as she remembered his response. Firm supple lips that explored hers, sent flutters into her belly, even though she had initiated the embrace. His hands were warm as they caressed her from her shoulders down her arms. A riot of sensations awakened a lustful ache and she found her hands wandering near his waist band. She teased and enticed him using her mouth and hands in tandem. Soft moans sounded in her throat and the kiss became more active and passion filled.

The buzzing of her phone broke through her memories and Siona pressed her lips together in irritation.

"Yes, Mom," she said, forcing her voice to sound like she was really awake. "Already? It hasn't been twenty... oh it had? I need to brush my teeth and I will be down."

She threw back the covers and flung open the door to the closet. She grabbed a clean pair of jeans and sleeveless mock V-neck. Siona somehow managed not to fall and give herself a concussion as she tried to both brush her teeth and pull on her clothes in tandem. Her hair, well she decided that she would just have to brave her mother's wrath, as she took the necessary five minutes to smooth her hair into a tuck and pin-up. She cursed mentally as she began to push and pin her hair forward, almost in a side puff, pinning the ride side higher than the left. She dropped at least a dozen hair pins as she rolled the hair from the top and around to the right and neatly finished it off. She grabbed her purse and ran.

Siona sprayed on some perfume as she exited the foyer of the hotel. She bent down to adjust the strap on her sandal and when she stood, watched her parents' car pull into the drive. She smiled tightly as she pulled open the door and slid into the back seat. A cup of coffee was handed back to her and she took a long drink before making her accusations. Her mother beat her to the punch.

"From the sound of your voice, I knew you had fallen back asleep and would need coffee. So, no my darling, I did not make you panic unnecessarily."

"But you knew I would rush around. You could have given me ten more minutes," Siona said, and hated the fact that sometimes she still whined at her parents.

"What I know, is that your aunties want to spend time with you and will not care if you are made up or not. I also know your cousins will be there after lunch and will undoubtedly drag you away," her mother said calmly. "In addition, your schedule is all screwed up, but the best way to get on track is to get up. I know you were smart enough to take a few acclimation days when you get back home. So embrace the sun and be with the rest of us normal people."

Siona muttered many obscenities under her breath about her mother not being normal people as she drank her coffee. By the time the coffee was gone, they pulled into her aunts drive way. She hoped the caffeine would kick in quickly. She was used to a full eight hours of sleep and didn't quite know how she would function on only half that amount.

She got out of the car and pasted a smile on her face. She walked into the house to find it bustling and filled to the seams again. While she understood that hundreds of cousins and other family relations would be continually appearing for the next few days, she did not understand how everyone could keep each other's names straight. It seemed like everyone but her could keep the others separate. She waved at the cacophony of greetings and made her way into the kitchen to get another cup of coffee.

"Look, it's Chrissie's girl," her Aunt Sadie said and pulled her into a warm hug.

Siona focused on keeping the smile on her face while her great aunts manhandled her with greetings. She finally made through a round of introductions for people she wouldn't remember tomorrow and almost to the coffee machine before she was pulled away.

"Don't tell me you're one of those who fill up on coffee before having real food," her Aunt Sadie clucked. "Come get this plate, child. I know you're in the city with those skinny freak models, but if you lose any more weight you'll blow away with the wind."

A heavy plate full of scrambled eggs, bacon, greens, biscuits and gravy was thrust into her hands. Siona breathed through the smile on her face. She was more of a croissant and coffee breakfast type of person, since breakfast usually came around 5 p.m. at night. She tended to eat her heaviest meal around midnight. Lack of sleep plus slight revulsion at all of the greasy foods, made her look for the darkest, quietest corner possible.

"Oh damn, they hooked you up," Keith said, relieving her of the sagging plate and gave her a tall mug of coffee.

Siona gratefully looked at him over the rim.

"Keep practicing, I almost believed that smile you gave when Aunt Sadie greeted you," he said. "I am surprised to see you here. You were out with your new *friend* until almost six."

She grunted and shrugged. Her phone buzzed in her pocket and she smiled. Siona resisted the urge to look at the text, knowing she would be asked more questions.

"It was a good talk," she said. "He works at the most state of art planetarium in the US right now; I had a lot of questions."

"About his job?"

The disbelief was all over his face. It didn't even change as he shoveled mouthfuls of food into his face at an intriguing rate that fascinated and, yet, horrified her.

"So that was him texting you just now?"

"I don't know," Siona shrugged it off. "It would be rude to stop chatting you up just to answer a text from a stranger."

"Well? Are you going to check?"

"It's probably just my job. Mathias is probably still asleep. He didn't have a family reunion to get up for," she muttered. "And it will have to wait anyhow. Apparently I am in high demand because I cut out early last night with you two. Not like I won't be here for a few more weeks to be around."

Keith nodded as he put an even more impressive mouthful of food away. She looked at him in amazement until he met her gaze.

"What?"

"Somehow, you are the most disgusting, yet clean eater I have ever seen," she said. "It's almost like watch a slow motion train wreck. I know I should look away, but I just can't."

"You don't date much do you?" he asked.

"Oh leave her alone, you pig," Kayla said, walking into the hidey space. "You eat like a slob. Don't be all passive aggressive and push it back on her dating life. Which by the way, as a single person, you have no room to talk. You better find someone soon or the gay rumors are going to surface again."

Siona loved her even more, when her cousin handed her another fresh mug of coffee.

"Aunt Sadie, is asking for you again, Siona," Kayla said. "I'll get the details of your date later."

Siona plastered a wider smile on her face and went out into the thrall of her aunties and uncle. There were many questions flung at her of the usual sort: job, relationship, future plans. As she answered, she shot a look to her mother requesting help. The traitorous woman, left to get food, and her plea went unanswered, and she spent the next forty minutes talking about herself. The call of nature saved her and she excused herself, much to the laughter of her relatives.

"Like the word 'restroom' is all that formal," Siona muttered to herself. "And for the record, *you're* the ones with accents."

Her phone buzzed again. Siona reached down near her ankles and fished it out of her pocket. Two missed texts from Mathias. None from work.

Good Morning Siona.

Would you like to meet up for coffee before braving your relatives?

She grinned.

Sorry. I was telling most of my life's story to my aunties. I would have rather gone for coffee with you. You are up early.

She stared in the mirror as she washed her hands, and wondered how long she could hide out in the bathrooms. A loud banging was the answer.

"Other people need to use the *restroom*, too," Keith bellowed.

"You're a jerk," Siona hissed at him, as and she passed by wiped her dripping wet hands on his shirt.

Kayla rolled her eyes and nodded her head toward the kitchen. They grabbed food off of platters and sat at the small table in the corner. Siona sighed in contentment as she bit into piece of bacon.

"I don't know how the Auntie's managed to make bacon better, but this is amazing," she said with a blissful eye roll.

"They bake it," Kayla said. "Anyhow- you need to spill."

Her phone buzzed and she looked down at it.

I know a great place for ice-cream. Maybe later?

That sounds amazing, and hopefully it's more than twenty minutes away from my family.

"You're texting with him already? Girl you better spill it, or I'm going to tell the aunties that you're seeing someone here. If you thought they were invasive before…"

At least twelve of their older cousins/aunts/relations burst raucously into the kitchen. The act of fifty-ish year old women gossiping and giggling made Siona watch them in amazement. She watched her mother amidst the group of women, but acting like she had never seen her before. She and Kayla weren't noticed in the corner alcove.

"Come on, you have to share. Crystal is finally here," one woman said. "She doesn't know all about your crush. I mean, I've been emailing her every week, but still she has to hear about it like you tell it."

Another round of giggles sounded.

"Oh, he is muy caliente. This man makes me think of things so naughty I need church after I see him."

The laughter got even louder and Kayla let out a low groan.

"Oh, girl. Stop. Just because you watch one telenovela doesn't mean you can actually speak any Spanish. Just tell us about your last encounter."

"Okay, fine. You heifers hush and let me talk. Let me bring y'all up to speed."

"The one calling them out is Auntie Lynn," Kayla whispered. "The ring leader speaking the horribly bad Spanish is my mother, Kinetra. And apparently I am about to hear things to scar me for the rest of my life."

The two girls shrunk further back into the corner where they sat at the table. The older group of women moved further into the kitchen and gave Lynn the floor.

"Well you all know that I have been taking those deep water aerobics lessons, keeps the pressure off my knees," Lynn said. "And all the time I been going there, this man named Jamal has been there too. He is tall and good looking dark skinned brother. By that I mean, the body on that man, makes a girl think about all the things she could do to him. With her tongue."

The girls flinched as the noise got louder and the story continued.

"Come on, get to the good parts," Siona's mother urged.

"Okay, this fine ass man keeps coming in to do the free swim every time we have class. Jamal makes it a point to walk by and say 'hi' to me each and every time. So, I decided that I need to ask the man out."

The women giggled and made rude noises.

"Keep going," the crowed urged Lynn on.

"I wanted asked him to come over for dinner and cards. Except the crazy women I take class with are some kind of haters and were trying to make conversation with him too. There is this skinny… lady there. You know the kind- hips so sharp they would cut up anyone trying to get closer? Well she likes him too and has been making noises to interrupt our conversations," Lynn said. "So I take Ki-ki and D.R. here to have my back while, I am asking out this tall, sweet, drink of espresso."

Siona exchanged bewildered looks with Kayla, who held a finger to her lips. Siona gave her a scowl that she hoped her cousin interpreted as 'tell me everything later' glare.

"These two here, come in like they own that darned pool and flaunt themselves all over," Linda said. "I mean, trying to with their scrawny butts. But Ki-ki and D.R. took care of it all. When we got in the pool, they made sure to accidentally shoot their workout noodles at those other broads."

"It worked," Kinetra said. "They got a face full of water and made all sorts of noise."

"So Jamal comes in, looking fine as ever. And watches these crazy women flailing all around with those noodles and laughs as he walks by them, but winked at me. And damn, doesn't that man just salt my greens. So I decide that I was going to finally just him over," Lynn said, drawing out the story.

Siona nodded her head toward the hall, trying to indicate they should be trying to escape the story. From the theatrics her Aunt Lynn was putting into the story, she knew it would go places that neither she nor Kayla wanted to hear. Her cousin shook her head, and they both shrank farther back into the alcove.

"Unfortunately I had the bad luck of him not being done with his lap swimming. Instead of leaving after class, I decided I would take a dip in the hot tub and wait for him. These hens over here, start making a fuss, when he comes over to tell me good bye and have a nice day. So I ask him out," she paused for effect until urged to tell them. "Anyhow this man said yes, and the noise got so crazy, the lifeguard had to ask them to be quiet. As Mr. Tall Dark and Gorgeous leaves he gave me a look that made me so hot, I had to bump Ki-ki away from the hot water het nozzle."

Siona's eyes grew wide in horror as her elder females howled in laughter.

"You should have heard the sounds she made as he walked away," Kinetra said. "He turned around to watch her. Then she and D.R. started fighting about whose turn it was to be on the nozzle."

The women cackled and laughed as the story grew louder and sexual innuendo turned into a contest to make the raunchiest comments possible. Siona's face blushed red and Kayla looked horrified.

"We should run," Siona whispered as quietly as possible.

"If we make any movement, they will pounce on us like prey," Kayla whispered back. "Give it a minute and they will leave." Siona stayed still, feeling more and more like vomiting as the women in her family gave her a new sex education. The additions from her mother, forced her to find the happy place in her mind. Finally, one of the great aunts called out to them and the group left.

Siona and Kayla bolted for the back door. She was certain that if they had walked through the living room, they would have been trapped once more. They made it to the safety of the car, and only when they had gotten down the block did they realize they had left Keith. Siona sent him a quick text telling him to be get outside and ready to leave and as they drove around to pick him up, sent a quick note to her mother as well.

You are a bunch dirty old women. I don't think I will ever get those stories out of my head.

71

Her phone vibrated immediately.

You don't stop having sex after 30 dear daughter. I saw you cowering; did you hear all of the good parts?

Siona groaned and shook her head. Keith jumped in the car and asked no questions. Her phone buzzed again.

By the way—if you thought that was dirty, you have a lot to learn. Aunt Ki-ki said to tell Kayla that the four of us will sit down soon.

She relayed the message to her cousin and then had to explain everything to Keith, who proceeded to gag. The rest of the ride to their shop was quiet.

Chapter 8

The next morning Mathias stretched and sat up. A smile creased his lips as he thought about Siona, yet again. Before his brain had awakened fully, he had his phone in hand and sent her a text. They hadn't been able to meet up the day before because of her family reunion stuff, but they had texted back and forth. His phone rang, startling him into almost dropping it. Just seeing her name was a rush.

"Good morning," he said his voice slow and sweet.

"Yes, I suppose it is," she answered. "I don't know how many more days of this waking when the people are around I can handle. My mother called an hour ago and forced me to see sunlight. Funny, she never mocked me like this in New York. Being around her family brings out the worst in her."

"Well, I am glad to hear your delightful voice. So how does meeting up tonight sound? It's going to be a clear, dry night—perfect for a drive-in."

"It sounds great, although, this is where I have to admit that I have never been to a drive-in."

He chuckled at her suddenly shy tone and shook his head. His perfect and flirty response to her was interrupted by a banging on his door.

"Mathias. The guys want to hang out tomorrow. We're going to G's for a cookout. Your sorry ass is expected to be there. We all know you are on vacation, so you have no excuse."

He heard Siona's giggles and sighed. He opened his mouth to talk to her again, but was met with more banging.

"Mathias, did you hear me?"

"I'm fairly certain most of Flint heard him," Siona said laughing even harder.

"Nathaniel, I'm on the phone. Yes, I heard you and I will think about tomorrow," Mathias called back through the door. "I already have something to do."

"You have plans? Open up, man."

He had no intention of opening his door and let Nathaniel snatch up his phone. While he couldn't be certain those events would happen, he erred on the side of caution. He heard a disgusted sigh from the other side of the door.

"Bring the chick too. We all want to meet her."

The peals of laughter on the other end of the phone contrasted with his groan.

"Since you heard all that...," he said.

"Sure, I will come along and meet your friends. Nathaniel sounds like he will be an interesting person."

"Thaniel is an ass," Mathias said as a reflex. "So, now that tomorrow night is all planned, do you still want to meet up and go to the movies tonight?"

"Absolutely," Siona said. "I can fill you in on the latest family reunion horrors."

"Horrors? You've only been here for three days. What on earth could they have done to you already?"

"I will tell you the gory details tonight. I don't think I want to have to relive them more than once. What are we going to see?"

"There's a remake of a classic comic series," Mathias said with a grin. "I don't expect it to be much better than the movie they did a few years ago, but I loved the comics as a kid, so I have to watch it."

"Sounds like you and Keith would get along well. Or maybe not. Do comic books and role play games have much in common?"

He smiled widely; glad that she couldn't actually see it. She had opened the door for many more talks about comic books.

"Bring your cousins along."

The invitation slipped out of his mouth before he could help it. He shook his head in disgust. He really didn't want extra bodies there, especially ones that might come between them. Mathias wanted all the alone time he could get with her. The thought rang soberly through his mind. He actually looked forward to seeing her. Already. But those feelings might wear off in another week.

"I'll ask, but I doubt they will. They have some event in a week or so. They have to finish up costumes and what not for their show."

He wasn't sad to hear that news.

"Do you want me to come pick you up?"

"Where? With my family? Goodness no. Oh, wait. I will be at the shop. You can pick me up there," Siona said. "I'm sure Keith and Kayla want to look your over or stare at you, anyhow."

He laughed and hung up after good-byes. Since there was nothing else on his plate, due to his own enforced vacation, Mathias called and made plans to take his grandparents to the Flint Farmer's Market to walk around and have some lunch. He had made it a priority to spend time with them each week since he had been sixteen. He dodged the very candid questions from his grandmother about his dating life. By the time his visit was over, he had gotten sage advice, a couple of warnings and a reminder that no one wanted to be alone.

Mathias kissed his grandmother's cheek and smiled as he walked away. A brief flicker of a thought crossed his mind. And then he squashed it. It was too soon to tell.

Mathias looked over at Siona again and grinned. Her face was lit up with delight. He wanted to know what she had expected when he said drive-in. He explained to her that the US-23 Drive-In Theater was one of the few in Michigan that had managed to stay open since its first show in 1952. It had even managed to upgrade to the digital system, which kept it going after so many others had to close.

"So we're just going to sit here and watch the movie. In your car?" she asked.

"No, actually I brought chairs and a blanket, so we can sit in front of the car. That way we can see the stars too."

She actually clapped her hands together and he resisted leaning over to kiss her. Her enthusiasm was infectious. And it turned him on.

"This is neat. Did you bring popcorn?"

The greedy gleam in her eye made him chuckle.

"There is a concession stand back there. Come on, let's get crazy and once we settle in, we can satisfy all the junk food desires you had from childhood."

He wasn't disappointed when she leaned over and kissed him. He even managed to ignore most of the cheering from a group of teenagers. When they broke for air, he trailed his fingers down the side of her face. With a clench of his gut, he knew he was falling for her. And for once it didn't scare him. Which in itself should have scared him, but he just went with it. They walked hand in hand to the concession stand and ordered their snacks. He noted they had completely opposite food tastes, and they went back to enjoy the movie.

Or make quips at it, as it were. She caught on quickly to the groans of the others around them. Mathias quietly began to give her the history from the original comic books and explained why so many people were mocking the screen.

"If they expected it to be crap, why come and see it?" she whispered back.

"Because comic book fans are die hard. We have to see for ourselves that it's a piece of crap. Word of mouth just doesn't work," he whispered back.

They both had fun mocking the pseudo-science of the film.

"The radiation from the portal would have just killed them all," she whispered.

"But then the movie would have been over an hour ago and we would grasp at straws for things to do."

"We could have made out more," Siona said with a dismissive shrug.

Mathias grinned, until she met his gaze and gave him a sultry wink. He leaned in and pressed a light kiss to her lips. She leaned in closer and placed her hand on the back of his neck. Loud cheering from the teens next to them, made him pull back."

"Your place or mine?" he asked.

"Mine," she said. "No roommate waiting."

They packed up quickly and drove to her hotel.

Mathias stretched in bed and grinned. Siona snored lightly next to him. He couldn't wait to tease her about it. He blessed the dark out curtains of the hotel; it was almost nine in the morning. He knew her sleep schedule was messed up, but he couldn't complain about being part of the reason why. He scooted out of bed quietly and walked into the bathroom. He looked at his reflection in the mirror and shook his head at the big goofy smile on his face.

Okay, the facts. I am enjoying the heck out of this vacation fling. The guys would never let me hear the end of it, if they knew more. Yes, I am taking her to meet them tonight," he whispered to himself. "Last night was pretty amazing and I really didn't expect it to end like this. The whole thing is pretty crazy. Stop overthinking this and go out and make the most of the rest of this time off.

His thoughts were interrupted as he heard the bed creak and brushed the morning mouth away. Walking back into the room, he looked at a tousled looking Siona. Her smile reassured him, and he climbed back into bed with her.

"Good morning," he said.

He wrapped his arms around her as she leaned over and kissed him. The contented rumble in his throat sounded as she deepened the kiss. He leaned back and let her run her fingers down his chest, over the slight grooves between the muscles in his abdomen and up to his pectorals. She played with his flat nipples until he sucked in a breath as they became hard buttons under her fingers. She pulled back and looked at him and gave him a wink.

"Good morning. Do you want to grab some breakfast?"

"Maybe after," he said, and slowly kissed up her neck.

Siona melted into his embraces as Mathias kissed her again slowly, moving from her lips down the side of her neck and to her shoulder. He loved the sound of her giggle as his lips moved over her collar bones and he nipped the sensitive hollow they created.

"Ticklish?" he murmured.

"Yes, but I doubt a tickle fight is what you really want to happen."

He conceded her point as her fingers made a slow path over his shoulders. He shuddered as she kissed all over his chest. Mathias lifted her chin, and then covered her mouth again with his and swallowed her sighs. He was fairly certain she was trying to drive him crazy as she moved closer and slid her leg down and over his. She ran her hands over his chest again. And then slowly lower.

Her grip was soft, but unyielding as she slowly touched him. Mathias relaxed and enjoyed her gentle stroking. He liked that she met his eyes and winked at him. With every ounce of self-determination he had, he slowly removed her hand. He ran a finger up her side. So far he hadn't minded that she had led the adventure, but he wanted to take control.

"You're right; a tickle fight seems like a waste of energy," he rasped out. "And while I certain enjoy your touch; I have a better plan."

She began to laugh as he lowered her to the bed and began to excite her as he kissed her body. His body responded as Siona exhaled a lusty sigh. He continued the slow exploration up and down her curves as she scored her nails down his back as he held himself above her. He moved lower again and traced around her navel with his tongue. Mathias kissed his way down to the top of her thighs and slowly used his tongue to caress her wet heated sex. When his tongue found her core, her hips bucked and she arched closer to him. Each flick of his tongue caused her body to shiver and with a final long lick the orgasm broke over her and she swallowed a keen cry.

Mathias's hand shook as he covered his length with smooth latex. She matched his grin as he came into her in a sure smooth stroke. She wrapped her legs around his waist, pulling him closer and began to move against him. He gave a husky grunt as she squeezed tightly around him and picked up the pace. Tension deliciously coiled deep in his belly as he timed each thrust, driving the pace faster and passion higher. She gripped his forearms and he noticed her limbs began to shake from the intensity of the orgasm crashing through her. Her pulsing against him sent him over the edge and Mathias's low growl signaled his completion and he fell against her. They lay kissing in each other's embrace as the trembling slowed.

"That was a pretty great way to greet the sun," Siona said, pulling the coversheet up.

Mathias watched her roll over onto her side. He smiled at the sensual look she gave him from her pretty hazel eyes. He met her smile and trailed a finger over her cheek and down over her shoulder. She met him halfway as he leaned in and kissed him again.

"What are your plans for the day?" he asked when the kiss broke.

"Well, there is another meet up with the family that I am expected to be at. My mother has made it clear that no one was particularly happy that I fled yesterday before lunch as even served. Even though it was her and Aunt Kinetra's fault. There have also been some not so hushed conversations about me acting too good to stay with them," she sighed. "At least I know Kayla and Keith will be there. It will give me some reprieve."

He smirked as she shivered when his hands ran down her side.

"What time is this lunch?"

"In an hour," she said. "And I cannot be late. So as much as I would love to continue to make out with you, it will have to be later."

Mathias sat up with a nod. Moving away from her was the only way to get away from the temptation. Siona sat up as well, but on the other side of the bed.

"I do kinda feel compelled to let you know something."

"Really? What is that?" he said in a low sexy voice.

"I'm not particularly good at parties," Siona admitted. "We're supposed to go over to your friends tonight. I'm going to be awkward and probably goofy."

Mathias leaned over and kissed away the worried look.

"It will be fine," he said. "They will mostly behave."

"Mostly?"

"Nathaniel will make some stupid comments, it's his defense mechanism," he said. "The rest will be okay. Flora will probably be there too, so you won't be the only woman."

"Somehow that won't make it much better," she flopped back down the bed. "I don't really have many female friends."

"It will be fine," he said, leaning over to kiss her temple. "If it gets bad, we'll just leave and find something else to do. Now get showered before you are late and your parents coming looking for you."

"And find you here?"

"Doing things to their daughter that they wouldn't appreciate seeing," he said,

"Yeah, that's the way to get me motivated to shower," she grumped.

"And so sadly, I must leave."

He kissed her one more time, and then left before his tease became truth.

Chapter 9

Siona groaned and flopped on the bed in the hotel. The day had been longer than she thought possible. After the exciting night with Mathias, she had expected the giddiness to carry her through another day of meeting family members whose names she would promptly forget. She had been wrong. Lunch with her mother and the rest of the crazy family was loud as she had expected. What was not expected was that Kayla and Keith didn't show up — at all. Nor did they answer their phones. So Siona spent the next seven hours in the bosom of her family. A hot sweaty, sticky, crushing, overly ample bosom, filled with questions and a quiet judgement about every aspect of her life. She felt absolutely drained and when her phone rang, she wanted to throw it. Only Mathias's name on the screen stopped her.

"Hi," she mumbled.

"Wow, you sound like you are either ready for a drink or you…actually you just sound like you need a drink full of liquor. The harder the better."

She laughed at his assessment and rolled over onto her back.

"It was the kind of day that reminded me why I dread traveling all over for a family reunion. I almost called up my job and cursed them out for giving me so much time off. My cousins ditched me without warning, so I just spent eight full hours with my extended family," she said. "I now have all the words to express just how happy I am to be an only child. How was your day?"

"Don't be jealous when I say quiet," he chuckled.

"Too late. But at least one of us had a torture free time. I think I never want to see another person again."

"Are you up to another get together?" he asked. "There will only be six or so of us."

"Are there drinks full of liquor there?"

"There will definitely be beer, however if liquor is what you want, we can stop and get some," he said.

"What kind of beer?" she asked. "I am a snob when it comes to my drinks. Well at least beer, if you are serving something from a can forget it."

"Travon is going to love you," he said, laughing harder. "He makes his own microbrew. See you in ten?"

"Make it forty-five and you have a deal," she countered. "I have to wash the residue of my family off of me."

"On the other hand, I could just come join you in the shower."

"The night is young," Siona laughed. "How about we go hang out with your friends for a bit; I need something to restore my faith in humanity. Then we can figure out what else we want to do. I am going to shower and you can handle yourself whatever way you see best as you imagine me with water running over my very naked body."

She hung up her phone with a wicked grin before he could respond. Other than the fact of having her own space, staying at a hotel also gave her the benefit of twenty full minutes of steaming hot water to relax under. By the time she got out, she felt ready to go and hang out for a few more hours. Dressing was easy only because of a limited wardrobe choice.

"They don't have to like me that much," she grumbled to herself as she stared at her three choices. "I'm only here for a minute. Still it would be nice not embarrass myself or him. This is ridiculous. The sundress is the best choice. No wait. Capris and t-shirt will be fine."

Siona talked herself through being okay with her simple outfit. She grabbed some coconut oil and quickly pulled her hair and retwisted it into spirals. A knock at her door made her jump, even though she knew Mathias was on his way. She opened the door and smiled at him.

"You are beautiful."

She blushed and pulled him in for a kiss. He tasted like mint and she enjoyed the slow exploration of her lips against his. His warm hands fit against the small of her back. Siona pulled back when they came up for air. She wanted to keep kissing him, like they had just invented it, but they had places to be.

"You are the sexiest woman I have ever met," he said with a grin.

"Thank you," she said skeptical at the look her gave her. "What?"

"After the reception for saying you were beautiful, I just wondered what calling you sexy would earn," Mathias said.

Siona smiled and ran her fingers up and down his arm in a lazy pattern. She met his eyes with a heated smile. Her fingers trailed lowered. She brushed against his navel, twice. She met his lips again, but slowly gave him tiny kisses that traced his mouth. She made her way up to his ear.

"A stiffie you have to conceal from your friends," she whispered and stepped back.

She watched his eyes snap open and broke into peals of laughter. She grabbed her purse, phone and room key.

"Ready to go?" she asked brightly. "Let me guess, it will take about twenty minutes to get there."

"That was mean," he said.

"No. Thinking me silly enough to melt for compliments was mean. I didn't kiss you because you called me beautiful," she countered. "I kissed you because you're hot and I want to do naughty things to your body. With my tongue."

She laughed as his mouth opened to say something and then snapped shut. Her raunchy auntie had been useful after all. She waited.

"You *are* beautiful," he said.

"I know," she said. "Your friends are waiting. Can you walk? Or do you need another minute? Cold shower?"

The muttering made her laugh more. She was pretty certain she caught the words "hell-cat" and "show a stiffie" in his less than audible rant that lasted until they got to his car. He opened the door for her and she winked at him as she sat.

"Better?"

"Absolutely, beautiful."

He returned with a smile that stole her breath. The car ride was uneventful, because Siona forced herself to behave. She really had wanted to caress his inner thigh as he drove. Her phone buzzed in time to distract her enough. It was a text from Kayla begging her forgiveness for abandoning her for the day. She took the opportunity to tease her cousin with next to no details about going to spend her time with Mathias, and then shut her phone off.

86

They turned off the main road and were enveloped in warm darkness.

"Are you taking me to a kissing spot or to your friends' house?" she teased.

He pulled into a small drive way and put the car in park before he looked at her.

"Damn, woman. Can you behave?"

"I did," she insisted, but placed her hand on his leg. "I managed not to touch you the whole way here."

She eagerly kissed him back as he pressed in with a sexy smile. He cupped her face in his hands and slowly slid his tongue against hers. His mouth consumed hers and she felt heat flare off of her. She pressed her hands against his chest and got a heady rush as she felt his heart race. A loud pounding at the drivers' side window, scared a strangled scream from her and she jumped back. A smiling face winked at her, and then was gone.

Mathias's head had whipped around and a soft stream of extremely creative curses flowed from his mouth. His warm hand on her leg helped to settle her. Siona touched his hand and he looked over at her. He smiled and brushed her cheek with the back of his hand.

"That was my best-friend. I *will* kill him if you want."

His offer made her laugh and helped her to shake off the last of the adrenaline.

"Ready to go meet the rest of them?"

Siona shook her head and waited as he walked around to open her door. She grasped his hand and walked toward a small cabin. Out of habit, she looked up and exhaled her wonder. The skies were beautifully clear.

"I am completely jealous that this is your friends view every night."

She appreciated Mathias stopping with her, giving her time to take it in. After a few moments, they continued their walk, but walked around the exterior to the back where the deck was. Four bodies were already there, around a fire pit in the middle of the deck. She immediately spotted the face responsible for her scare.

"About time you got here," he crowed. "I didn't think you two were coming up for air."

"That would be Nathaniel, my former best-friend and roommate," Mathias muttered. "My offer still stands just let me know. The others will help me hide the body."

Siona giggled, she couldn't help it. The displaced passion and adrenaline left her giddy. The rest of the introductions were made in short order. The tall man to her left was Travon; the man to her right was Gregory and next to him stood his girlfriend, Flora. She hadn't expected how relieved she felt to see another female. She gripped Mathias's hand a bit tighter as he introduced her to his friends.

"And I even set up my scope earlier, because I am that awesome," Mathias said and pointed to the corner of the deck. "And by my scope, I mean the newest toy the planetarium got delivered today. I haven't even put my hands on it yet. It's even tablet controlled. Let me go get you a drink."

As he walked away, Siona couldn't wait to grab the tablet. Her plans changed when the other woman came up to her with a smile. Flora was at least a head shorter than her, but had a welcoming aura. She, too, wore simple capris and a tank top.

"What horrible thing did Nathaniel do to you?"

Siona returned a grin at the soft feminine voice.

"He caught us kissing in the car and pounded on the window."

"That man," Flora huffed. "He is just soft in the head. The rest of them are normal. Mostly. They just keep him around because he just won't leave."

She liked Flora right away and felt tension melt away. Mathias returned and handed her a beer.

"You need to smell it first and then take a taste," he instructed.

Siona inhaled and smiled. She took a small drink and nodded her head.

"Pale ale with raspberries?" she asked.

"Keep her," Travon called from across the deck. "Even Flora couldn't call it the first time."

"Because your first batch sucked," Flora countered. "You've been working on this one for months."

"And you know nothing about beer," Travon countered.

"Because I drink wine. Which is why my wonderful boyfriend is going to serve me a glass of a chilled rose, some time tonight."

"Yes, he is, but would love if you could help him bring food out of the kitchen," Gregory chuckled.

Siona grinned as Flora sighed loudly but walked in to the house. She wasn't alone too long before Travon came over.

"So, what do you think about the brew?"

"Well the appearance was light amber with about two fingers width of a persistent frothy white head, lots of bubbles, and an amazing trail of lacing. The aroma is pale malts, raspberry and bitter hop. The taste closely follows the aroma with the hops forefront in taste, but is balanced well with the pale malts. There is a slightly sweet taste from the raspberries. Finish is pleasant and rightfully bitter on the palate. There is a nice dry mouthfeel with a clear finish."

"Are you sure you want to date Mathias?" Travon asked. "That is the best description of my beer I have ever heard."

"I'm sure you need to leave," Mathias said, wrapping an arm around her waist.

Siona laughed and took another sip. She hadn't even heard Mathias approach. She mentally thanked herself for giving in and going to a craft beer fair with her co-workers. The tiny bit of knowledge she had gleaned was worth it. She looked up at Mathias and winked.

"He may make a great beer, but you have a planetarium."

She met him halfway and didn't think twice about kissing him deeply. She shivered as his hands rubbed her arms, but definitely wasn't cold. In a few moments, she forgot about everything but the man holding her close.

"Hey, you two. Time to untwist your tongues," Nathaniel shouted from across the deck. "Dinner."

"Does he do everything loudly?" Siona asked as they broke apart with a smile.

"Yes," Mathias said. "I'm surprised he didn't come over and pull us apart."

They made their way over to the table and took seats. Flora and Gregory finished bringing out dishes.

"Flora said I couldn't go over and interrupt you or she was going to block access to any porn for the next month," Nathaniel informed them as they sat. "No way I was coming anywhere near you two lovebirds."

Siona met Flora's grin and laughed.

"Thank you," she mouthed across the table shadows.

Gregory held up a glass.

"New friends and old, welcome. My home is yours, enjoy. Cheers."

"Cheers."

In that moment, Siona became aware that she would be leaving in two weeks. And decided she really didn't want to. She had friends back home, but nothing this cozy. She gave herself a mental shake, reminding herself that she didn't actually know much about these people and they were probably like everyone else. She told herself to live in the moment and just have a good time.

The next few hours were more fun than she expected. Since she was normally so awkward around people, it was refreshing to be able to chat and laugh with a small group. Dinner was fresh fish caught from the lake behind the house and grilled, along with veggies and more beer. Chatter was light and friendly, other than the few jibes tossed around from the guys.

During a pause Siona wandered over to where the telescope was set up and bent over to take a look. She sighed and loved seeing the stars. Every single amazed her again. When she looked up Flora had joined her.

"The testosterone was getting pretty thick," Flora said. "They are arguing about some ball game, and since I don't care, I left. Anyhow, it's nice to have another woman to chat with. And since Mathias hasn't given up any details, I hope you don't mind sharing."

"I met him at his star party a few nights ago, and he has been kind enough to show me around Flint," Siona said. "I went to my first drive-in, last night."

"Oh, so you're into the skies too?" Flora asked.

"Astrophysicist," Siona confirmed.

"And you drink beer," Flora laughed. "No wonder he fell so fast. He even set up an enticement for you over in the corner."

"Yeah, I've been dying to get my hands on his instrument all night," she said.

"I heard that," Nathaniel called out.

"Shut it," Flora warned.

"Right, boss-lady. I will behave."

Siona walked over to the telescope and looked it over. She picked up the tablet and looked over the wireless telescope controller app. She pushed a few buttons and then frowned. She tried a few more and then groaned.

"What's wrong?" Flora asked.

"It won't sync," she moaned.

"Give me a minute," Flora said. "I'll be right back."

Chapter 10

Mathias walked over to the Kegerator to refill his glass. He still found the name amusing; he thought Travon was full of shit when he had first used the term. Gregory joined him and then looked over toward where their women stood, ogling the telescope. Their heads were close and they spoke in low voices, with just a hint of excitement

"When do we get the good details about this amazing woman that you are dating?"

"When you don't invite Nathaniel?" Mathias retorted with a chuckle. "Next run I might have to beat his ass for the stunt he pulled earlier. He is my best friend, but some days I want to strangle him."

"As you do," Gregory said, taking a healthy drink. "Where did you meet her?"

Before he could answer, there was a groan from the corner. His head snapped up and he watched Siona move her fingers over the tablet. Even though her face was half hidden in the shadows, he could see the upset. Before he could make a move, Flora walked toward the house at a rapid pace and before he could blink, had turned back around and returned to where Siona waited. In a few moments, a soft glow from a laptop illuminated the women's faces as they peered intently at the screen.

"What's going on?' Gregory asked.

"I don't know," he answered.

As then men watched, Flora grabbed a cord from the back of the telescope and plugged it into the laptop. After her fingers flew across the keys, she nodded at Siona who tapped on the tablet. Mathias was instantly jealous that he wasn't the one to make her smile like that. Then she leaned over to look through the scope and his gaze dropped to her ass. He met Flora's eyes as she walked back by.

"What was that all about?"

"Who ever thought they set up the tablet to sync with the telescope forgot to refresh the ports, so I had to go in a do a manual override."

She breezed into the house and then back out to stand with Siona.

"You know she dumbed that down for you, yes?" Gregory asked.

"I'm sure she did, and I still didn't understand half of what she said. The tech guys said they set it up. I haven't even put my hands on it yet."

"Well crisis averted. Now spill, because I have never seen you like this about a woman."

"She's only here for a few weeks," he said. "We're just enjoying hanging out. And to answer the earlier question, I met her at my star party the other night."

As he started giving details, he noticed Nathaniel and Travon moving in closer to hear what he said. Mathias gave them the light versions of the dates and no information about sleeping with her. He watched his friends absorb the stories with nods and then shift the conversation back to the plans for the rest of the weekend. *Back to the Bricks* was running, and they had been attending since 2005 when it had been a one day show. Flash forward to the present and the event lasted five days, hosted thousands of cars for the cruise and many hundreds of thousands of people.

"Are you going to bring Siona?" Gregory asked. "I'm sure Flora would love the company."

"When did you get Flora to agree to come?" Travon asked.

That started a light debate between the friends, where good natured jabs were thrown at each other. They laughed more and when Mathias looked over, the women were still chatting lightly and looking through the telescope. As much as he would have preferred to be by Siona's side, he gave her space for the time being.

A few hours later, Gregory was ready for them to leave and had no problem booting them out. Mathias was thankful for it, because other than dinner, he hadn't been near Siona at all. While he was thrilled she had hit it off with Flora, he wanted to spend what little time left he had with her alone. The possessive thought again stopped him short for a moment. He was getting attached more than he liked. He mentally shrugged and reminded himself that in about nine days, their fun would be over.

"Ready to go?" he asked as he approached the corner of the deck where the scope stood.

"Sure," Siona said brightly. "Want me to break down the scope for you? She sure is amazing."

"Go ahead; you're probably itching to caress her curves. I know I am."

Mathias decided that flirting early would serve as foreplay. He stood by and watched as she deftly took apart the telescope and put it away in its case. The big smile she gave him was worth not doing the work himself. They made their way back to the small group on the other side of the deck and said their good-byes. Mathias comfortably put his arm around Siona's waist as they walked back to his car. He had just stored the case in his trunk when Nathaniel came up.

"Hey, do you two want to come hang out for a while?"

"Why?" Mathias asked cautiously.

"Mom and Dad are home tonight, and are probably watching for lights to come on so they can swarm me."

"We will pass," Mathias said getting into the car. "Have a good time."

"You're just going to leave me to suffer with them?"

"Karma."

Mathias drove away, expecting Nathaniel to move or get his foot run over. He drove towards the city, and looked over at Siona.

"What would you like to do now?"

"As much as I would love to have you spend the night, I have to be up early. I'm taking a road trip with my parents tomorrow," she said.

"Okay," he said. "By the way, I didn't notice anything awkward about you tonight."

Ten minutes later he dropped her off at the hotel's front doors. He had offered to walk her up, but she wisely pointed out the folly of it. Instead she gave him a kiss sexy enough to heat his blood, and said good night.

He made it home, where he found Nathaniel in front of the T.V. holding a game controller in his hand, yelling at someone on the other end of his headset. Mathias grabbed a headset and the other controller and spent the night shooting aliens.

Despite waking early, Mathias had no intention of sitting home and moping because Siona was off on trip with her parents. Visiting family was the whole reason she even came to Michigan.

However, it did leave him with a huge gap in his schedule. He got up early, went for a run; something he rarely did as a man and came home to shower. He came out to find Nathaniel dressed like he was going to a funeral.

"Country Club with the parents?" Mathias guessed.

"You can come with me and alleviate my burden," his friend made the request with hope in his voice.

"I'm going to see Pops and Granny."

He almost felt bad when he saw his friends' shoulders dejected slump. Then he remembered the pounding on the car window.

"We can go for beers after," he offered. "Suck it up for a few hours and just remember to keep quiet."

It only took Mathias ten minutes to get dressed after he had shoved Nathaniel out the door. He pulled into his mother's drive way and was surprised to see her car. He figured she would have been at work. It should have been his first warning.

Mathias walked into the house and opened his mouth to call out, when his eyes landed on a familiar face.

"Jordan."

"Mathias, it's good to see you. I'm really glad you came."

He allowed himself to be pulled into his older brothers arms. After a second, he returned the hug. It had been a long time.

"Mathias?"

He could hear the shock and pleasure in his mother's voice. She rushed over, probably to make sure they weren't about to get into a fight. The smile that covered her face as she looked at her sons erased the tired lines from around her eyes.

"Hey, Ma," he said as she hugged him.

"Thanks for remembering to come," she said.

"Hi, Mathias."

The soft voice pulled his attention back to his brother, where his sister in law stood. She still looked the same. Her dark mocha face was framed with a short chic haircut and her eyes were still pools of black velvet. His brother put his around his wife's waist and held her close. The tension in the room rose, and Mathias realized they were waiting for his reaction.

"Hi Ebony."

He waited for the feelings of hurt and disgust to surface. They didn't. Mathias was surprised to realize, he felt absolutely nothing. Nothing, but happiness at seeing his brother home and safe.

"Well, let's go out back and eat. You came just in time," his mother said quickly. "The ribs just came off the grill."

He figured she was making sure he had no time to change his mind and leave. He followed her to the backyard and went to greet his grandparents. They sat at the closest table and waved him over.

"I'm glad to see you got over that nonsense and showed up," his Granny said as he hugged her.

His grandfather shook his hand, and Mathias saw the smile of pride he was given. He almost was ashamed of his behavior from the years past. He didn't realize how much of a strain he had put on his family by holding a grudge.

Lunch was loud and chaotic and the most fun Mathias could remember having in a long time. All six siblings were there and many stories were told from childhood, causing shrieks of laughter and denial of events more than once. His mother took great delight in telling them the oft repeated story of Mathias and Jordan and the Easter Eggs. Having four sisters was a big challenge for the boys and after enough teasing and torture, they decided to teach the little girls a lesson. Why, no one could remember, but the boys had hatched the plan to get their sisters to crack raw eggs on their heads.

They dyed raw eggs in lovely pastels for their sisters. For their own eggs, they had died them a bright orange, so they wouldn't make a mistake. The big scene was set, and Mathias had called the sisters to the backyard. He told them that whoever cracked the egg over their head and peeled it first could have his basket of candy. Jordan joined in too, to make it look real.

Their mother came out when the yelling started, and found all six of her children there with egg yolks dripping down their heads. In their haste to execute their brilliant plan, the boys forgot to boil their own eggs.

"I almost forgot all about that," Mathias gasped as he laughed.

After a few more stories, his grandparents excused themselves to have a rest. Before he knew what was happening, his mother had ordered his sisters to clean the table and go inside for dishes. Ebony had gone in with them, leaving him alone with his brother.

For a few minutes they sat quietly with tension filling the air. Mathias wasn't sure how to start a conversation with his brother. They weren't kids any longer, and he didn't really know the man who sat across from him. Jordan held out a beer to him and then quickly retracted it.

"Sorry. I forgot mom said you don't drink."

Mathias grinned and stuck his hand out.

"I just usually don't drink around here because of my promise to Granny. I wouldn't mind having a drink with you."

"Thanks for being here today," Jordan said. "It means a lot. To both of us."

"Mom asked me to stop by," the lame excuse was out of his mouth before he could stop it.

"Mathias, when are you going to let it go?" his brother sounded frustrated. "Ebony and I have been married for six years. You had a school boy crush on her. You went on one whole date. I didn't steal her from you; she was never interested in you as a boyfriend."

Mathias sat back and took a sip. Not to be pissy, but because when he thought about what caused the rift between him and his brother; he knew it didn't matter to him any longer. He had had a huge puppy dog crush on Ebony and was hurt when she dumped him for his brother. What struck him in the gut was that even as he thought about the past, the only woman on his mind was Siona. When he compared what he felt for her and Ebony, he nodded at the truth of his brother's words. He had never loved Ebony; he had just felt possessive of her.

He wanted to be able to blame it on his werewolf nature, but the reality was much more simple. Mathias was a year younger than his brother, and had always looked up to him as the great example of everything. Ebony had been a year older him and they had gone to one movie. They had run into Jordan and a group of his friends at the theater. He had seen the looks pass between his brother and his date. Ebony had thanked him that night, but told him she wasn't interested in dating him.

When Jordan started dating her two weeks later, Mathias had been furious. He had picked at his brother until they had a fight. He just knew with his werewolf strength, he would win. His second surprise in two weeks was the ass beating he got from his brother. It started a cycle of antagonizing and threats until Jordan left for the Navy, but not before he and Ebony had eloped. Mathias swore off relationships and blamed them both.

"I have let it go," he said, coming back to the present. "You and Ebony make a great pair."

Punching his brother in the face would have been much less surprising than his words. Mathias smiled and took another, longer sip.

"Okay, don't look at me like I'm an asshole, but when did you get over it?"

"It really doesn't matter, Jordan. The point is it's done. I let it go. I've wasted enough time and too much of my energy feeling like you wronged me. I'm tired of being mad about a school boy crush. You're right and I'm sorry."

He did his best not to laugh as his stunned brother took a long drink. Mathias watched him finish his beer and set the bottle down before facing him again. He met his brother's eyes.

"Who is she? I need to meet my future sister-in-law"

Mathias choked on his beer.

"What?"

"You look just like me and that's the look I had on my face when I realized that I wanted to marry Ebony," Jordan said.

"It's not that serious," Mathias protested. "She's only in town for a few weeks for her family reunion. We've just seen each other a few times."

"Her name?"

101

"Siona."

"Where did you meet her?"

"At my last star party," Mathias muttered.

"She's into astrology too?"

"She's an astrophysicist."

Mathias's head snapped up at the howl of laughter coming from his brother. He caught the bottle tossed his way and sat back to drink it, while his brother laughed himself out. There was no pretense his brother tried to control himself.

"Let me get this," he gasped out. "I come home, hoping to make peace with you because Ebony is pregnant. Instead I find out the girl of your dreams showed up at one of your parties and you're now dating. The best part is you think you're willing to let her go at the end of her vacation?"

"Ebony is pregnant?"

Mathias met his brother's eyes.

"Congrats, man."

"Thanks. You're the first one I've told," Jordan grabbed another beer and held another out. "Now, tell me about this woman."

Chapter 11

Early morning found Siona sitting in the back of the car pretending to read her tablet. Instead she worked on hiding a grin that would surely get questions flung her way rapid style. Mathias was keeping her company via text on her road trip. Never once had she considered traveling to Michigan would mean dating someone, but she certainly enjoyed her time with Mathias. New York was a city that had events happening all the time and she hadn't thought about what she had been missing.

After her few dates with Mathias, she realized she spent too much time at work and not enough time having fun with the friends that she did have. She looked at the cover to the newest edition of the popular telescope magazine and futilely swiped through the pages. Her eyes looked out the window at the rapidly passing scenery.

"Where are we going, again?" she asked.

Her mother turned from the front seat to face her with a huge smile.

"Idelwild," she said. "My uncle Elijah lives up there. He is my Daddy's brother. When I was growing up, we visited up there every summer. Because of Daddy's job at the plant, we were lucky enough to get two weeks of vacation. His family still owns the summer cottage that overlooks a clear lake. You are really going to love it, Si. There is so much family history up there. You are going to love talking to your Great Uncle, he is an amazing man. Actually he's the black sheep of the family, and has some great stories to tell."

Siona had heard about the summer hamlet a few times from her mother, but in all her visits to Michigan, she had never visited the rural area. The last time she had seen her great uncle was at the Williams' family reunion and she had been ten. All she remembered is that it was loud, fun and had a lot of card playing that she was not allowed to be a part of. She was curious as to what it would entail.

"Is it like a resort?" she asked.

"It used to be, but so much more. My Daddy loved to tell me how some of the finest African-American musicians of the 20th century played there. Really famous artists like Aretha Franklin, Peg Leg Bates, and Jackie Wilson came and gave amazing performances for all the summer residents. Imagine being in the presence of such famous people. It was called the 'Black Eden', you know," her mother said with pride laced in her voice. "They still have an annual jazz festival, but we missed it by a few weeks. Actually now that your dad and I are retired, we might start coming out during the summers to attend the music festival."

Siona nodded, still having a hard time wrapping the rural lifestyle around her head. She was a city girl through and through. While her family had taken camping trips as vacations periodically, she had actually appreciated the vacations to theme parks and resorts much more. While she teased her mother about the "20 minutes away" rule that worked in Burton, she got the lofty reply that it was only two hours over the twenty minute time. Her mother had filled most of the ride with excited chatter.

"We would ride horses, fish and hike through the woods picking wild berries my Granny would bake into pies," she said. "Every day we went to Williams Island to swim at the beach. It was amazing to see such a robust community there. It was even bigger when my Daddy was younger and we grew up hearing the stories. Of course now it's much quieter. All the clubs and dance halls that used to be the hottest places to go and be seen closed years ago.

104

Actually they were before my time even. But it's slowly starting to make a comeback."

It seemed like her mother was telling a great story from the history books, but she wondered what they would find when they arrived there. Even though her grandfather had died when she was just a little girl, Siona had warm memories of his deep voice telling her stories her mother at a young age. At the time, she couldn't believe that her mother had ever been so young and had giggled incessantly. She only remembered bits and pieces, but those she had were cherished because her mother reminisced about him fondly.

"So we're going up the family cabin?"

"No, we will go back tonight. It's only a couple hours ride," her mother assured her. "Are you going to spend more time with Kayla tonight? Even though you are forever running off, I'm glad you have made a friend to hang out with."

Sure, my cousin who is done being patient with the lack of details I have been giving her. Of course it helps that she is really busy to be a nag, because I have the feeling if she had the time, I would have been tied down to a chair.

"I've enjoyed my time with them. We're a lot alike," Siona said. "For instance, we're still both horrified about hearing Auntie Linda talk about her man."

Her mother laughed so loud and hard, that her father gave in and asked. Siona's face flushed red as her mother retold the story—not sparing any details. Especially about the text. Her father chuckled as well and she shook her head.

"Did we forget to have the sex talk with her Crys?" her dad asked.

"Traitor," Siona hissed at him.

"I know we seem positively ancient, but we are still healthy and active," her dad said, meeting her eyes in the rearview mirror.

"And this is where I put in headphones and leave you two alone."

Siona thought about sending Mathias a text, but stopped herself. Everything with him had moved super-fast. She had no regrets, their dates had been fun and the romance had been amazing. She also knew that there was a time limit and the idea of how to continue picked around the edges of her brain. Her phone buzzed.

I just found out you aren't coming over today. I swear if I don't get details soon, I am telling everyone here that you've been dating a local boy.

She quickly responded that she would give them a blow by blow later that night when she returned. Siona put in head phones, leaned against the door of the car, and closed her eyes to sleep through the rest of the trip.

An hour later her mother's voice penetrated the fog of sleep and she sat up. Somehow she had expcted more. Instead she looked around and what appeared to be nothing. Lots of trees as they drove down the streets, but everything was depressed looking. She tried to imagine it as her mother had told her.

"What happened?"

"The Civil Rights Movement. All the famous acts learned that they could make more money going to the big cities, and the crowds followed. We were just looking for inclusion," her mom said. "After the sixties things started really slowing down. When I came up here as a kid, it was more for the community than the big names. But now with the music festival, it is slowly coming back. Half of the problem is it's been forgotten. This was a big deal and yet most people in our culture know nothing about it."

Siona could do nothing but shrug; she had family in Idelwild and had never heard anything about it. She couldn't imagine how it would look packed with people enjoying food and music, but made a mental to note to return the next summer and drag her cousins up to experience it with her.

106

"Okay, we are going to have lunch with Uncle Elijah and then stay and chat until he is done," her mother said.

Siona shrugged. There was little chance the small town had anything of interest to pull her away. As she watched the trees flying by, she noted the lack of buildings.

"Where are we going to eat?"

"Oh, Aunt Sadie packed a big basket of food for us," her mother gave her a wink. "I'm pretty sure she packed up all food Kinetra and Linda made. She says they are too heavy handed with their spices."

They pulled up to small cabin, after winding through the woods a bit on a dirt driveway. Siona helped her father carry in the supplies as her mother knocked on the door. Uncle Elijah invited them in, but stopped Siona as she passed. He held her at arms length and looked at her. He gave her a huge smile.

"I am glad to meet you again, Siona," he said in a soft voice.

"Nice to you meet you too, Uncle," she said.

She helped her mother set up lunch and listened while she ate. Her uncle told many stories about her grandfather ranging from his youth to when he had become a new father, to her own mother. Siona was getting comfortable and about to drift off in her own thoughts when her named was called.

"Siona, your mother tells me that you work at the big fancy planetarium in New York."

"Yes, I do research there," she said.

"That is so good. You're the only one in the family to take after my own dreams," he said. "I always wanted to be an astronaut."

He grabbed her attention with his simple admission.

"And here I thought I was the only space lover in the family," Siona said, warming to him more.

"No, I have always loved it. I even got my degree in astronomy twenty years ago."

"Uncle Elijah, why did you ever tell us?" her mother asked her voice pitched in surprise.

"Well, that was the year that Ellie got real sick. I only had one class left to finish. I had already applied for graduation. She passed half way through the term. I never attended the ceremony," he said. "It was enough for me to know I got it."

"What was your favorite class?" Siona smiled at the wizened man.

"Classical mechanics," he said. "I loved the ideas of the motion of bodies under the influence of forces or balanced forces due to equilibrium."

She nodded at him, "Quantum mechanics for me. My goal is go back in another year or so and start to work on my doctorate. So far my colleague think the theory is backwards, but what do they know?"

Her Uncle laughed and then pushed back from the table and stood.

"I've got something to show you. Chrissie, we can move to the living room where it is comfortable."

Siona watched him shuffle down the hall, and then turned to help her mother take care of the remains of lunch. When her uncle made it to the living room and settled into his recliner, she joined him again. He turned on a small table lamp and motioned for her to lean in.

He opened his hand a showed her a chunk of rock that was attached by wire to a necklace. It looked rather ordinary to her.

"The other thing most people don't know is that I worked for NASA," he said.

"What?" Siona asked in surprise.

"I did, in the early sixties. I was one of the best brrom pushers they ever had. Partially because I also loved science, and I was asked a lot of questions about probablities and euqations," he said with an affirming nod.

"Wow, so you were there when the moon launch and landing were going on?" she asked. "I'm sure that had to be an exciting time."

"Sure was, a bunch of fancy, important people around all the time. I even helped one of those delgate people find his missing wallet," her uncle glowed as he told his story. "I didn't think much of it at the time, but then a year later he visited again. Boy was I surprised when he remembered who I was. Anyhow, that's just a long story for another time. He gifted me with a piece of his moon rock. Broke a piece off right in front of me."

As Siona watched he held up the rock on a chain and then pressed it in to her hand.

"I want you to have it," he said. "Something this important should only go to another stargazer."

"Oh uncle, I can't take your moonrock," Siona insisted.

"Sure you can," he said. "I'm not going to live forever. I would rather know it went to a good home, rather than some stranger. You will enjoy it like I have."

She went over and hugged her uncle tightly. It was a touching gift and she was surprised to find herself misty eyed. The rest of the visit was just as fun. She heard many stories about her grandfather's side of the family, including stories about her mother when she was younger. Siona was sad to find that their time had come to an end.

"Y'all need to leave," her uncle said. "I go play cards with Ms. Joy down the road every night. Thanks for coming to visit."

They said good bye and left the old man preparing for his date. As soon as they left the drive, her mother turned around to face her with a grin.

"Yes?" she asked.

"You do know that piece of rock or whatever he gave you is fake right?"

"It was a sweet gift," Siona said defending her uncle.

"Honey, it was a lovely gesture, but I have heard no less than a dozen different stories about his time at NASA. Though that one was new. Let's see," her mother began to tick the jobs off on her fingers. "He's told us that he was: the fourth astronaut on the Apollo for the actual moon landing, he's has also been secret service keeping mission details secret, he was also the head trainer for the atronauts. I'm surprised he said he was a janitor this time isntead of the delegate. Anyhow, enjoy the trinket."

Siona put on the necklace. Even if her uncle made up the story, she would cherish it.

"No matter what, at least he worked at NASA," she said.

Her mother snorted and then turned back to face the front. Siona picked up her tablet and began to read through a book she had picked up at the airport store. It held her attention for about five minutes before she felt her eyes get heavy.

Siona's phone buzzed against her leg, waking her. She sighed; she had forgotten to give Kayla the heads up about her arrival time. Mathias's name was on the display, she grinned.

Can you get away tomorrow afternoon? I have something I want to show you, but it doesn't start until after dark.

She texted back an affirmative answer and then rolled her eyes at herself. She knew that she would be giving up all the good details that night. She was going to need her cousins to cover for her once again, and she knew it would come with the cost of telling them everything.

She sent Kayla a quick text, and drifted off.

Chapter 12

  Mathias woke and stretched with a smile on his lips. After a daylong draught, Siona was coming back into town. He knew he had it bad, the long overdue talk with his brother had already confirmed his feelings, but he had stopped thinking that something was weird about it. There was no reason not to embrace actually liking someone. In fact, he had also decided that would work through his fear of relationships. He wanted to be with Siona, and if it meant long distance until they could figure out all the details, he would work with it.

  As he lay in bed just letting his thoughts take their own course, a plan began to form in his mind. He only had nine days left with Siona and he wanted them to be as memorable as possible. He tried to use their forced hiatus as time to really sit with himself and figure out what he really wanted. Nathaniel pounded on the door, opened it without invitation and leaned against the frame. He grinned as his friend gave him a look of supreme indifference.

  "Are you going to get like Gregory?"

The sneer was so thick it almost had tangible form.

"What? Happy because I have found a woman that keeps me in a state of amazement?" Mathias asked. "And before you insult her by making a crude joke about sex, Nathaniel? I will take your throat out on our next run. Don't be stupid."

"Woah. You've got it bad.

"I sure do, and it's fucking fantastic," he chuckle, looked over, and gave his friend a wink. "Just wait until it happens to you. You're always so cocky and removed, but when you meet the right one, you will get sucked under just like the rest of us."

He laughed as Nathaniel left his room in a hurry, crossing himself and reciting a fake chant about staying true to his single self.

After a leisurely shower, he got dressed and headed over to see his grandparents. He needed to get supplies while he was at it. Mathias hoped he would be able to act casual around them, they were fairly perceptive. He promised he would tell them later, when the details got settled.

"Will you finally just tell me where we are going?" Siona implored.

Mathias grinned at her. "It will completely ruin the surprise and we are almost there."

He turned into the drive to the park, knowing that she really had no idea where they were. He pulled into a lot containing two other cars and smiled at her.

"Ta- da. We have arrived."

"So now you can tell me where we are?"
"We are at the Headlands state park in Emmet County, along Lake Michigan and west of Mackinaw City," he said casually.

"We drove four hours to visit a state park?

"We brought our telescopes," he said.

"The stars aren't going to be different just because we are four hours north," she grumped.

"We can drive over the Mackinac Bridge," he offered.

The sour look on her face made him chuckle, which turned the look more hostile. He took a breath, got his presentation voice ready and looked at her.

"We're actually in an International Dark Sky Park. It's one of only six in the U.S. and ten in the world," he said. He grinned as the look on Siona's face changed. "It was designated as a Dark Sky Park by the Arizona-based International Dark-Sky Association in 2011 after experts measured the amount of light in the area, and found that it offered a clear, unaltered view of the night sky. Tonight we will get to see a glorious offering of stars and planets that are usually drowned out by light pollution from city streetlights and buildings."

He was pressed against the side of the car door as Siona unbuckled herself and threw herself into his arms. He had no idea what she was trying to say, as she alternated between giggling, squealing and trying to kiss him. Mathias let her excitement affect him as well, and waited until she calmed down.

"I don't know if I didn't know Michigan had a dark sky park or I just forgot," Siona gushed. Her excitement filled the air around them. "I can't even begin to describe my excitement right now."

"The stars won't really be visible until around ten-thirty tonight, but I wanted to have a chance to look around and grab up a prime viewing area. I even brought the necessary supplies."

He was tackled again, but this time, there were no words spoken. Instead Siona pressed her lips to his and gave him a heated kiss. Her tongue slid against his in an open seduction and she ran her hands up and down his chest. Mathias closed his eyes and lost himself in her touches and kisses. The sounds of a running engine broke through the haze and he sat back.

"That was you being excited, huh?" he chuckled. "This is the best gift anyone has ever given me."

"Keep it in mind as you wear the backpack," he suggested. "It has all of your equipment. For the next few hours."

They walked around the four mile loop of the hiking trails. The weather was agreeable and they enjoyed have free time to talk about everything and anything. As the evening set in, they decided to go set up their spot, but after walking along a narrow rocky path, they found the general area fairly crowded and decided that walking further down toward the beach might offer them more privacy.

He held Siona's hand as they made their way to the water's edge. They set up chairs, a beach blanket, and sat waiting for the stars to come out. Mathias unpacked the picnic his grandmother had insisted on preparing. He unclipped the soft collapsible cooler from the bottom of his pack as he set up. He shook his head as he saw enough to feed six people.

He pulled out a container holding grapes, blue berries and strawberries. The next was filled with raw vegetables cut into bit size pieces. Cheese and crackers came next and then a container of hummus dip. He wasn't aware that his Granny even knew what hummus was. She usually stayed with simple fare.

"Is that Brie? I love it," Siona said, watching him. "The nice thing is it won't go all oily and nasty like Cheddar, from the heat. It will just get melty and yummy."

It wasn't lost on Mathias that everything was a finger food. They sat on the blanket in front of the shore of Lake Michigan and watched the sun set. He leaned over and tried to feed Siona a strawberry, which just earned him a look as she pulled away from him.

"I know it's supposed to be all romantic," she said. "But I really don't like other people manhandling my food."

"It was my Granny's idea," he laughed. "I am more than happy to let you feed yourself. If you get too chilly being next to the water, I saw a small hill not far back behind us. I also brought some blankets."

He lost her attention when a shooting star chose that moment to streak halfway across the sky. He agreed with her soft sounds of wonder, it truly was a beautiful location for stargazing.

"I'm pretty impressed with how many people are out tonight," she said. "I'm also glad we are far away from the families with little kids. Not that I mind them, but the idea of going blind as they play tag with flashlights tonight isn't my idea of fun at all."

Mathias grabbed two pair of binoculars from his pack and cleaned up their food. He handed a pair over to Siona. He had borrowed a good set of night sky binoculars for the trip. He had polled the his friends from other planetariums and they urged him to get something with strong magnification to resolve the thousands of light-points within dense star clusters, and it would also help them to pick out fine structure within galaxies.

"I am pretty sure I can see Saturn," she said.

Mathias loved the way her voice went up a few octaves and got breathy when she was excited. He picked up his binoculars and nodded in agreement at what he saw. He looked over as she laughed.

"You just nodded to me, in a dark park."

"And you saw it," he chuckled.

"Only because I was looking right at you," she said in a fake lofty tone.

"Can't say I'm upset that you spend just as much time looking at me as you do the sky," he leaned closer and punctuated his words with tiny kisses. "These were what my colleagues recommended. I'm glad they knew what they were talking about."

He finished packing up and sat next to her. Mathias enjoyed every second cuddling with her until the sun sunk under the horizon. As a special bonus, there was a spectacular lightning storm raging on the Wisconsin side of the lake. They were both amazed as lightning arced between the clouds and thunder rolled across the lake.

"I hope we don't have to cut our trip short," Siona said, moving closer to him as a gust of wind from across the lake chilled the air.

"It's going the other way, thankfully. Don't worry; I packed an extra blanket in case you get colder. Or…"

"Or what?"

Mathias took full advantage of their privacy and leaned her back to kiss her. He felt her warm body relax as they lay on the blanket in the sand. He slowly nipped at her bottom lip and tasted a mix of berry juice on her. Her tongue gently slid against his, enticing him to press closer. He broke the kiss away from her lips and slowly moved down her neck. He lightly traced her collar bone with his tongue and then back to kiss over his path.

A gasp, made him lift his head.

"Meteor."

The single word, caught his attention, and his caged his passion for later. Instead he decided to lie on his back and look up at the sky with her. The vastness of the sky was something he could simulate every day at work if he wanted to. Being under the real thing, in the absolute dark was a whole other experience. He clasped her hand, and they looked up as the meteor crossed the sky above them.

"I know some people say they feel small when looking up at the universe," Siona said. "But I just feel exhilarated. Look at all there is still to explore and learn about. It makes me feel like I am taking the baby steps of learning what we can find."

"I know how you feel," he said as he pressed a kiss to her shoulder. "It's that same feeling that always drew me to spend more hours at the planetarium than playing outside. It connected me to the feeling of bigger and more."

He loved how he could talk to her about his passion and she understood it perfectly. No feigned interest or flirty suggestions about making out under the heavens. Mathias was sure the other women had suggested it because it sounded sexy to kiss under the stars, but they never had been as invested as he was. However, Siona was different, and he planned to kiss her breathless while under a blanket of stars.

He released her hand and slowly began to run his fingers up and down her arm. He alternated between using his finger tips and the pads of his fingertips as he drew random shapes over her arms. He could feel the goosebumps as they sprung up. Still saying nothing, he continued to caress her, moving from her arm to her stomach.

First he played nice and kept his fingers on top of the fabric. But he wanted to feel the satin of her skin, and slowly ran his fingers under the edge of her shirt. He could feel her intake of breath as her navel pulled toward her spine. Mathias used his short clipped nails to draw light patterns on her skin. He followed the pattern with his lips and felt her gasp.

"Mathias," she moaned.

His brain noted that she got as breathy saying his name as she had when she pointed out the meteor. He knew that making love to her was not in the plans. They were in a public park with plenty of people nearby. Not to mention he vividly recalled how much sand could find crevices in naked flesh, from the one time he had gone skinny dipping.

Mathias's attention was yanked back to who he was with as she returned his exploration by running her nails over and down his shoulders. He looked down at her with a lustful smile.

"We have all night to be here, since it's open twenty-four hours," he said. "I'm going to have to behave; else the urge to drag you off to a hotel will ruin our star gazing."

"That's a tough call, but we only have one night here," she conceded. "But we will have at least a week of nights together in my hotel room."

He sighed as he lay back beside her and contented himself with holding her hand. She started up a new conversation, telling him how she had actually made it out to Michigan. He laughed at the antics of her HR department, silently thanking Kim and Tony for making her take the extra time.

Mathias opened his eyes feeling a chill ripple through his body. The stars and moon shone brightly down at him, unobstructed. Embarrassed he looked over at Siona and breathed in relief, as she had nodded off as well. The last thing he remembered was them trying to find their favorite constellations. He sat up and looked toward the general viewing area, which looked fairly vacant.

"Siona," he whispered as he leaned in to nuzzle her ear.

It took a few more attempts to wake her, and he felt bad.

"Come on sleepy sweets," he said. "Let's go back home."

She yawned loudly, but sat up. He began packing away the chairs they had never used. He packed up the blankets and cooler. He looked over to see Siona run her hands up her arms. Mathias took over the duty and pressed his lips to hers.

He looked up into the magnificent sky once again. He sighed and so did she.

"Thanks again for bringing me here," she said.

Mathias looked over at her and noticed her pulling a necklace from under her mock turtle neck. At the end was a rather ugly chunk of rock. It looked like slag to him, but he was curious.

"What is that?"

"It's a piece of moon rock," she said proudly. "My great uncle really did work for NASA, but he is also known for telling tall tales. So either he was in the Secret Service, or he was the fourth astronaut, or he got it at a garage sale. Either way, it was a sweet gift from him."

He must have scoffed a bit too much at her declaration. She pulled the rock and necklace over her head and handed it to him. Mathias's hand began to tingle the moment the rock made contact with his skin. Fire licked through him and he dropped the backpack with a grunt. He fell to his knees as the air was pulled from his lungs.

Siona shrieked but he put a hand up toward her.

"Stop. Get back."

His body twisted and bones snapped.

This isn't possible. This can't be happening. The moon isn't even full.

It was the last thought running through his mind as he fell forward, panting. Fur sprouted, covering him in a dense warm coat. His canine elongated and his body compressed into its lupine form. In a few moments, his body had completely changed. He took once step back, and his paw burned. Mathias saw the moon rock attached to the necklace, and moved away from it quickly. The remains of his clothes fluttered around him.

His sharpened night vision made Siona's panicked expression clear, but she made no sound. Suddenly his body clenched and fell to the ground, where blessed darkness took over.

Chapter 13

Siona looked at the prone form lying before her and picked up the rock at the end of the necklace. She put it back on and tucked it under her shirt. She paced in the sand. Her mind spun around at all of the possibilities and ramifications of what had just happened. No one was around and she didn't know if it was a good thing or not.

"I wonder which story Uncle Elijah was true. I bet he was a secret agent," she whispered in surprise and then looked over to her date. "Holy shit, he's a werewolf. No, did I really just say that? Werewolves aren't real, I mean, except for the one laying here at my feet."

As she stared, the animal gave a sigh and effortlessly shifted back to man form. She looked around in the darkness and realized that she couldn't see lights anywhere.

"Which is the point of a dark sky park, you idiot," she chastised herself. "Okay, what do we do now? There is no way I can carry him."

Because of their rambling cover-all-the-topics conversation and impromptu nap, they had stayed longer than most other patrons. Actually, everyone had left but them. She looked over at Mathias, and went to get a blanket out of the backpack for him. As she approached him, his eyes snapped open. His eyes seemed to glow with an inner light as he tracked her movement. Siona held the blanket out to him, but said nothing. Mathias stood, but began to shake uncontrollably.

"I think you should sit back down," she said softly.

He wrapped the fabric around himself and stumbled as he took a step.

"Mathias, please let me help you."
"Stay away from me, Siona."

She flinched at the brusque tone of his voice.

"I'm not afraid of you."

Siona tried to keep her voice gentle. She didn't understand the wary look he gave her. She felt no fear; she knew he wouldn't harm her.

"Stay the hell away from me with that thing," he snapped, but his voice was raspy.

"I already tucked it away. It didn't seem to affect you before. I think you need to be touching it," she said.

She ached watching him trying to get his bearings and balance. The scowl on his face was dark and intimidating, but she didn't feel it aimed at her. As far as Siona could tell, it was the loss of control, and the weakness he had to show. She had no idea of what to say to him.

"Dammit," he snarled.

Siona rushed to help him as he fell again. He pushed her hands away, and she ignored him. He pulled out of her grip and she watched helplessly as he once again met the ground.

"I'm going to help you get to the car. I know you are upset, but unless you plan to stay here forever…" she let her voice trail off.

"Fine," he sighed. "Make sure you get all the stuff too."

Siona gathered the backpacks, and then helped Mathias stand. He leaned against her shoulder, but she noticed he was noticeably less shaky as they walked. She was glad for the slow pace because trying to carry everything made her stumble herself. By the time they reached the rocky path that would lead them back to the parking lot, he walked under his own power. She wanted to talk to him about everything that had happened. She had so many questions, but instead forced herself to pack everything into the backseat of the car.

"Do you want me to drive?"

Siona wasn't sure why she asked. There was no way Mathias was balanced enough. His derisive snort brought her up short and she whirled on him.

"What was that for?"

"You're not driving my car," he said in a low voice.

"And if you pass out at the wheel? Before you try to tell me that you won't, you don't know if you will or not. Nothing like this has ever happened to you before," she said.

To her grim satisfaction, he stomped to the passenger side and yanked open the back door. He ruffled through the backpack and then opened the front door sat down with a huff. Siona decided that it might be okay for them to sit and have a chat. She schooled her face to be calm and turned to him. His glower didn't deter her. It was hard to be afraid when he sat there naked.

"You don't happen to have an extra set of clothes in the car do you?"

"No… well wait. I have swim trunks in the back seat. I thought we might want to go swimming," he said.

"Oh I would have loved to have gone in Lake Michigan," she said. "Too bad you didn't tell me to pack a suit."

"I forgot."

Siona looked over and him and couldn't decipher whether the look on his face was mad or embarrassed. She tried again to lighten the mood.

"Well, for all of the things I could have imagined happening tonight, this wasn't one."

She waited a few moments. He gave her nothing so with a sigh; she turned the car on and began to drive. Siona clenched her teeth as he grunted out directions until they made it to the highway and then fell back into silence. She let it go for about forty minutes before his attitude began to upset her.

"Mathias, are you really just not going to speak to me? Yes, what happened was a surprise, but I'm not freaked out."

"Well I'm glad one of us isn't," he said.

"I know it must be disorienting for you, and then again, I guess I have no idea what it is like. How long have you known? Was this the first time?"

A few more miles flew by. She glanced over at him.

"Siona, I really don't want to talk about it."

"How can you not? Don't you understand what this means? You are proof that we have been looking for. Most of us gaze up at the stars because we hope to find other signs of life. We spend years in research and working on theories for decades just for the possibility that there is more out there than just us. Heck most of us die before we get a chance to find out if we were correct," she said. "There is more life out there."

"Theories and research don't endanger a group of people just trying to live their lives," he muttered. "Exposing the fact that we are real does."

"Are you kidding? Your existence means that there is even greater potential for alien life to occur as well," she said. "It can easily breakdown the all the doubters and people who just can't believe it would be real and show undeniable proof."

Siona tried really hard not to let her enthusiasm get out of control. She realized that for Mathias it was having his biggest secret exposed against his will. He obviously knew about his condition and had kept it secret. She thought about the few words he had said, and realized he was worried for his group as well. She let more miles pass, before trying to talk to him again.

"Is the changing on the full moon thing real?"

"Yes. Normally," he grunted. "Apparently real moon rocks have powers over us that no one knew about. Then again, no one I know has a real moon rock. Except you."

"You can have it," she offered. "You can put it in a locked safe and hide it, or better yet, take it to a lab and do some experiments on it and see if you figure out what makes it work on you."

"Because I can obviously touch it with no problems," he sneered. "None of us will be able to."

Siona didn't react to his tone and when she glanced over at him, Mathias stared steadfastly out the window. She exhaled quietly. She understood him being out of sorts, but still the venom in his voice was unsettling.

"Are you part of a pack? Is that what it is even called?"

"Yes."

"Is it a large group?"

She felt the heat of his eyes bore through her.

"Siona, I can't talk about this. Not with you," he stressed.

"Just me?"

"Humans dammit. Just stop asking me questions."

Siona huffed in frustration.

"You know, you were comfortable enough to sleep with me. Usually that's a pretty big sign that you trust a person."

"Sex has nothing to do with this," he said.

She sucked in a breath, surprised at the hurt his words caused. She focused on driving, trying to give herself time to process. While she understood that he was in shock, she didn't know how to reply without wanting to punch him in the mouth. Siona decided to act like an adult. One of them had to.

"Perhaps you are used sex being just a physical act, Mathias, but I am not. I came out here expecting a family reunion. Meeting you was a pleasant surprise, but I never expected more. And when we started dating, I knew it would only last a few weeks. Then I planned to go back to my life in New York with some fun memories. And despite how fast things went between us; it's because we have a connection. And you know that as well as I do."

After yet another snort, Siona was thrilled to see her hotel just down the street.

"Do you want me to drive you home or do you need to call your friends?" she asked.

"They should be waiting. I texted them on the way."

She pulled into the drive and parked.

"Look, Mathias..."

"Siona, I just need for you to go. Give me time to process this."

She opened her mouth, but the look on his face made her close it again quickly. He looked exhausted and panicked, and she wanted nothing more than to put her arms around him and offer some comfort. She got out of the car and returned the nod that Nathaniel gave her as they passed. Siona was proud that she managed not to cry until she got into her room and shut the door.

Two days later she had cried herself out. She had pled a stomach bug and stayed in her hotel. She was surprised just how much she had meant the words she said to Mathias, she did feel more than a connection. She went through the emotional rollercoaster and two pints of ice cream.

Siona finally decided that she was tired of smelling herself and took a hot shower. She used the hotel soap, because her own was to sweet smelling for her sappy mood. Her clean linens aroma therapy perked her up and as she smoothed lotion over her arms, she decided she was going to finish her vacation on a high note. A pounding at the door made her jump. She tried not to get her hopes up and she pulled the door open.

"We both know that you aren't sick," Keith said. "You got upset by your dude and you're sulking. Glad to see you are dressed in something that reasonably matches and don't smell like despair. Get your shoes and come on."

"Good thing I showered before you interrupted my pity party," Siona muttered.

She stood holding the door open, surprised. She stared at her cousin, wondering how to react. Kayla peeked around her brother and smiled.

"What he meant to say was that he would go kick Mathias's ass if you wanted. If you didn't, then we're going out. We need to grab more supplies and need the extra man power."

Siona looked at her family and a grin began to creep across her face.

"So, you came over here to make me work?"

"Hells to the yeah. You lug around that heavy case like it's nothing. We need a useful person helping," Kayla said. "And you need to get out of this room before you don't fit into the costume I want you to wear."

Siona looked at her cousins and began to laugh as she shook her head.

"Let me get this straight. Under the pretense of caring, you all told me: I'm going to get fat, I don't stink and somehow that surprises you. Lastly you need me because I am strong and can lift heavy things."

"Oh you did listen," Keith chuckled.

"This is supposed to make me feel better how?" Siona asked joining in the laughter.

"We're your family. We cut through the bullshit, call it like it is and exploit you all at the same time. Ready to go?"

She stared at her cousins for a moment more, feeling better than she had in days and grabbed her purse.

"Let's go," she said. "But expect me to whine about Mathias being a jerk."

"You won't be the first person to boo hoo about having their heart broken."

"Nice and subtle, Kayla," Keith grunted. "And I didn't boo hoo."

"Nope, torrent of tears was more like it. You should have seen it Siona, he moped, and checked his phone ever few minutes to see if she had called. For all that they say we women—stop snorting we are women, you asshat. You know what? You cried like a damn baby…"

Siona chuckled as she herded her arguing cousins out of her room, through the hotel and into the car. She was impressed that the no nonsense argument had continued.

"You guys can stop any time," she said. "I feel much better now."

She immediately realized her mistake as both Keith and Kayla, looked back at her over their shoulders.

"You thought this was about you?"

"You can tell she's and only child. Like we did all that to make her feel better," Kayla snickered.

Siona sat back as they began to laugh at her. And somehow, being the object of her family's ridicule made things better.

Chapter 14

Mathias woke up and stretched until his lower back popped audibly. He had about five seconds of early morning fog before the disaster of three nights ago before came rushing back through his memory. He sat up and his body adjusted again. The sounds reminded him that his body had been forced to change.

It scared the hell out of him. He felt like he did as a thirteen year old boy when changing was terrifying. Mathias's first experience was a blur, and he was happy for it. He had fought with his sisters and gotten whooped by his mom for hitting one of them. Anger pressed hard in his skull and made spots dance in front of his eyes, He stormed out of the house and began to walk with no destination in mind, and he just needed to move.

By the time he had calmed down enough to come back to himself, he was lost in an area he wasn't familiar with. Mathias had always had an overactive imagination and fear gripped him. He began hyperventilating and couldn't make sense of his surroundings. At any moment he expected a gang of thugs to jump out of the shadows and attack him. All the stories about the recent murders in Flint spun in his mind. His heart sped up and just when he thought he would throw up, everything went dark.

He came to in a field, with no recollection of how he got there. He sat up, and to his absolute mortification, he was naked. Under the inky black of the sky, young Mathias began to cry. After the tears stopped and the sobs quieted down, he stood and looked around.

"It's going to be okay."

The quiet voice startled a shriek out of him. He turned to face the speaker.

"Mr. Williams?"

"Yes, son. Let's have a talk."

"Why am I here? Why are you here?"

Mathias watched his counselor, ready to run if need be. The man didn't move other than to toss a small bundle his way. He found a pair of sweats and a hoodie. He quickly put them on, and turned to face the man with anger.

"Did you take my clothes? Did you touch me?"

He hadn't expected the gentle laughter.

"No, I didn't touch you. But I do have some answers for you. I can help you make sense of what is going on."

Marcus explained about his and Mathias's true nature. They were werewolves and that their race had mixed with humans long ago to help perpetuate survival. Over the years, especially through the Dark Ages, they became prey for the local, religious leaders to help set examples of Satan's wickedness. Their people fled for their lives and went into hiding. Which meant the lore was lost and newly born shifters had to go through life without knowing what they were.

Marcus's family had decided that their job was to find the lost cubs and bring them into their fold. In the past, they had gone through the insane asylums and jails. Currently, they looked for kids in juvenile detention centers. Marcus had taken it one step further and tried to find them before they got in the system.

As Mathias listened to the unbelievable story, he slowly backed up. He knew he would have to run away from the crazy man who stood before him. He kept inching away until he recognized a dark shape as his friend walking toward him in slow measured steps. At first he didn't believe his eyes, but as the other teen came closer, he held his breath.

"Hey, Mathias."
"Nathaniel? What are you doing here? Are you here with him?"

"Funny, I never would have expected you to be one of us. Although you did punch me in the face. Marcus, here, picked me out pretty easily because I am a trouble maker. We only found out about you from the sightings of a wild dog running the streets," Nathaniel said laughing.

Because his friend stood there, completely at ease, Mathias relaxed. Conversations were had and the next Monday at school, they were introduced to Gregory and Travon. It was unusual for one area to have so many lost cubs, but the boys didn't care. It just meant there was safety in numbers at school.

He had learned how to control himself when the moon pulled the worst of his temper to the surface. Along with the others, he learned how to work within their pack and what true loyalty meant. It gave him a sense of belonging he didn't know he was missing.

"Mathias."

Nathaniel's bellow shook him out of his headspace. It was his ten second warning before his door was opened and some two hundred pounds of supposedly best friend jumped on him.

"Let's go jogging."

He grunted, punched his friend in the ribs and then nodded. Ten minutes later and they ran the one mile trail at Flushing County Park. Mathias was glad to see he had full control over his limbs again. So far he hadn't had any side effects from his out of phase change. On their fifth time around the park, Nathaniel looked over at him.

"Want to talk about it?"

"No."

"What happened?"

"What part of 'no' don't you get?" Mathias snapped.

"The part where you asked us to come get you to drive you home and then told us nothing," Nathaniel said. "We're worried."

"I'm still trying to figure out what to do about it," he admitted.

They ran another mile in silence.

"I think you need to talk to Marcus about it."

"What? Are you kidding me?" Mathias stopped running and looked at his friend. "Why would I need to talk to him about it?"

"Because it's serious."

"That is the exact reason I don't want to talk about it until I have some kind of plan."

"You're trying to keep her safe," Nathaniel drank from his water bottle.

"No," Mathias scoffed. "It's over anyhow. This was only supposed to be a distraction while she was here visiting her family. She leaves soon. I'm just trying to figure out how to make sense of everything."

"Go talk to him," his friend pressed. "You are way smarter than I am, and if you have no idea how to fix what ever went wrong, you're gonna need some help."

He stared at his friend, wondering how Nathaniel had come across that burst of insight. He took a deep breath, intending to tell him what had happened. A splash of water in his face caught him by surprise. Mathias sputtered and then took off after his friend, following him to the car.

"Do you have to be a jerk all the time?"

"Nope, but you would get suspicious if I started in with the bleeding heart routine. Anyhow, I have to prep for a big interview later this week, so I need to go home. And you need to shower before you meet with our Alpha," Nathaniel flashed him a grin. "Before you tell me you don't want to talk with him, I texted him from your phone earlier and he is expecting you."

Mathias got in the car and punched Nathaniel as hard as he could in the arm.

"Thanks."

"You might ask him for some punching lessons too. Flora hits harder than you do," his friend laughed.

After a deliberately long shower, Mathias sighed deeply and got ready to meet with his mentor. He had to admit, silently and to himself only, that Nathaniel had a point. No answers had come to him, and the problem needed to be addressed.

He rode at what he thought had been an easy pace, and groaned when he realized the ride had only taken fifteen minutes. He was tempted to stop by Gregory's cabin as a delay tactic, but knew better. Sometimes Mathias was jealous at the tight knit nature of those from the pack who lived around the lake. It hadn't been by invitation only or anything, but when the last cabin had been up for sale, he had just graduated and had no money.

He walked up and loudly knocked on Marcus's door before he wussed out. Mathias exhaled a long breath, trying to calm himself down. He knocked again and after a few moments looked around. Since he knew Marcus was expecting him, he didn't understand the no answering. He started to walk down to the small community garden plot the residents had made.

"You looking for Marcus?"

He turned toward the husky female voice that called out.

"Hey, Tess," he answered. "Yeah, he is expecting me."

"Today? Really? He told me he was going to be out of town until next week's run," she said.

A mouthful of curses covered his tongue, and he wanted to spit them out. He bit his lip as he looked at the pack Beta.

"My mistake," Mathias said with a forced grin. "I was told he would be around."

She laughed and he rolled his eyes at her.

"Nathaniel set you up?" she guessed.

"Yes."

He bit the word off with more venom than he had intended. He wondered if his friend had known Marcus was going to be gone.

"What's up Mathias?" Tess asked.

He grasped for the words to talk to her, but came up empty. Because he didn't know just how serious the situation was, he was afraid of escalating it.

"I just had a situation that I needed to talk to him about."

"It is exclusively a guy thing? I'm pretty sure Gregory will be around later tonight."

Mathias paced a bit as he tried to find the best way to give her bits and pieces, but still keep her in the dark.

"How about we go grab a beer and sit on my deck and just chat," she offered. "From the look on your face, you need help figuring things out. I can either advise you as the Beta or as your friend. But I think you will feel better once you talk it out."

He nodded mutely and followed her across the yard to her home. He sat in the balmy morning, looking across the calm lake. Tess returned with two sweating bottles and handed him one. Idly he wondered if it was too early to drink, and then recalled the stupid saying of it being after five somewhere in the world.

"So I think the best thing is for you to just dump. I'll wait until you are done talking and then give you my take."

He looked at her as he tipped the bottle back.

"Last night, I took a date to the dark sky park up near Mackinac City. She had a piece of moon rock and it forced me to shift even though it wasn't the full moon."

He paused and waited for Tess to lose her cool. She sat calmly in her chair, waiting for him to give more. Mathias took a breath and nodded, at no one, and launched into the full story. He told her about their meeting, their dating and the great time he had been having. He also told her about Jordan, how they had fought and made up. He talked non-stop for about twenty minutes. When he got done, he sat back and took a long drink from the bottle.

Mathias realized that while it felt good to have everything out of his system, he was still nervous. The secret had been spilled and now he had to wait to see what would be done about it.

"So tell me about Siona," Tess asked in a quiet voice.

He smiled as he began telling all he knew about the woman who had invaded his life in such a short period of time. He retold about their dates and even how Siona thought some of the programs that he had created would be great at her own planetarium. As he talked, he realized a very important piece of information.

"And that son of a bitch lied to me. He never texted Marcus about me waning to talking to him. My phone has been off for three days, so I wouldn't have to ignore her calls of texts."

He watched Tess, who sat still in her chair on the deck. She looked thoughtful as she processed all the information from him. She tipped her own bottle up a few times before talking to him again.

"For one of our quieter members, you certainly get the award for the most amount of drama this month," she smiled at him reassuringly. "Well the problem seems to be whether or not we can trust her to be quiet with our secret."

"I doubt she would really say anything to anyone, but you should have heard her. Siona was so excited to learn about my true nature. She said it was a gateway for others to believe that alien life could even be possible," he said. "I expected—well, no, I never expected to have to tell her anything. She was going to be gone before the next full moon."

Tess nodded. "You were afraid of letting your pack know that it happened. What happened to that piece of rock?"

"She still has it, but she did offer it to me," he said, quick to defend her. "But that thing is dangerous to us. I barely had it in my hand before it took over."

"Can you trust her Mathias?"

He met Tess's honey colored eyes and felt the real weight off the question he had tried to avoid. He had gone rounds with himself trying to be objective. As he met the stare with a solid one of his own, he wavered. He thought he had been certain, but what if his shit behavior made her emotional and she talked?

"I'm pretty sure I can."

Tess stood up and reached for his empty bottle.

"Another?"

He nodded and she walked back inside. Mathias's thoughts tripped over themselves. He still tried to convince himself that he wanted to trust her, but there was some doubt. Tess handed him another beer and sat back down.

"I've heard your report."

Mathias sat up straight at the word. It sounded awfully official to him.

"This is what I think. First of all, thanks for bringing it to my attention. This is a serious matter, but also great information. Second, because you can't trust her I will take over from here," Tess said calmly. "I'm going to need more information from you, such as where she lives in New York and when she is planning to leave."

He started to protest and Tess flashed him a quick smile.

"Oh, don't worry. I won't do anything while she is in Michigan. I'll wait until she is back home and take care of it. I'll make sure to procure the rock and make sure our secret is safe."

The words were said casually, like every day conversation, but the intent had him on his feet before he could think.

"You won't touch a hair on her head," he snarled in a low tone. "She said she wouldn't tell, and I know her well enough to believe her."

"Before you said you weren't sure. You've known her for all of two weeks. She's a scientist; of course she is going to blab about us."

Mathias felt the growl build low in his throat as Tess threatened Siona.

"You better not get anywhere near her."

"I'm the Beta. I decide what is safe enough for our pack. You don't get to drop this kind of information on me, and then try to stop me from doing my job just because she's good in bed," Tess sneered.

"If you touch Siona, I'll kill you," he snarled.

Mathias felt the hairs on the back of his neck rise and his hands fisted. He towered over Tess who calmly drank her beer.

"Well then, have you figured it out yet?"

She should have just punched him and called him an idiot from the beginning. It would have been better than the smug smile on her face.

"You were never worried about her telling anyone about us. You were afraid to admit how much you liked her. I know you are just coming to grips with the whole brother date stealing thing, but suck it up. Siona means a lot to you. I suggest you fix things before she goes back home and you lose her forever."

Mathias sat back down and shook his head. He grabbed for his beer bottle and took a swig.

"You threatened her to prove to me how much I liked her?"

"You were being kind of thick," Tess laughed. "Think about it Mathias, you were quick to tell me about the moon rock and your shift. It took you a lot longer to describe your dates, in sickening detail, by the way. You are smitten."

He shook his head again.

"So you're not following her home?"

"Not unless she has a killer discount for 5th Avenue. Go talk to her. Apologize for being like Nathaniel. Make the most of the time you have left."

He stood up and smiled at her.

"Thanks, Tess. I appreciate the help."

He made it across the yard before she called out.

"Mathias?"

"Yes?"

"You might want to figure out how you want your long term relationship to work. Phone sex, sexy texts, video calls and such. It would be good to have a plan in place."

He hopped on his bike and rode away to her laughter. He needed to get back to his phone and figure out how to meet up with her.

Chapter 15

The next morning Siona sneezed three times in a row, paused and sneezed three more times. She had no idea that standing still, in a costume could make her so miserable. She also didn't really enjoy the earlier hours her cousins had talked her into. Five in the morning meant work was almost done, not just beginning.

"Bless you."

The words came from the silenced world outside and around her.

"Thank you," she muttered from deep inside the contraption binding her. "I still don't know how I let you talk me into wearing this thing while you made alterations."
A few moments of filing sounds later she got a response.

"I think you tried to say something, but I didn't understand it. You're pretty muffled behind that helmet," Keith said. "But if you're complaining, just remember you are the one who didn't give Kayla all the good details the other day."

Siona grunted in reply. She figured her cousins had stuffed her into the bulky thing so they didn't have to hear her complain about Mathias anymore. Granted, it would have been much easier to complain about the man if she could have actually told them the reason for his brush off.

"The nerve of that man to think I would spill his secret to anyone," she muttered to herself. "Why would I possibly betray him and his pack? It makes no damn sense. I understand that he might have been nervous about it all, but when it comes to the survival of his kind — I'm the enemy? Like I would go around running my mouth about what happened. Stupid man. What the hell, are we in fourth grade, you don't just stop talking to someone and hope they go away. Although I guess he can, because I am going away in a few days."

She tried to understand it from his perspective. The whole situation was quite scary. Siona knew that she wouldn't at all have been happy if some necklace made her involuntarily do something. On the other hand, she didn't think she would have jumped to the conclusion that betrayal was the first thing on her boyfriends' mind.

She stopped her thoughts and mulled over the fact that she referred to him as her boyfriend. She grumbled at herself, not wanting to admit how much she had grown to like him, but not able to deny it either. Her biggest hope was that he would get over himself and talk to her before she left.

"Are you still brooding in there?" Kayla's voice asked. "I kind of think this is some kind of crap, to be honest. First I hear next to nothing about your dates with him. Then you come back from your wet dream of a date and you two are fighting. I missed all the good parts. I should have tied you to a chair and made you spill."

Siona tried to nod, but was afraid that the motion would pitch her forward. She had no idea which character she was supposed to be and didn't care. The armor over the legs at least had hinges that would allow for walking without too much of a problem. The body suit was surprising light, until you got the chest plate. Kayla had spent hours putting in colored LED tape to make it light up in a specific pattern. Siona had to admit the glowing effect was awesome. The shoulder guards were bulbous and overly large and she groused about them a lot as her cousin adjusted them.

"Don't ask me," Kayla had said when questioned about their size. "I didn't design the thing; I am just making a reproduction of it. Apparently she uses it to ram her enemies in one of her power ups. Anyhow, do you have any problem rotating your arm around?"

Siona moved her arm with ease and gave her cousin the thumbs up. She sighed as she realized that her hand was encased in some kind of arm cannon, raised her other hand to give the positive sign. She stood thinking over the events for some time later, until Keith came over with a box.

"Food break," he said.

Siona waited while Kayla slowly pulled off the costume pieces. Each one was solidly made and fairly light by itself. Together it weighed much more than she had expected. She took a deep breath when it was finally off.

"How the heck do people walk around all day in contraptions like this?" she asked, mopping her forehead.

"Well for that character, there are variations on the costume, including a plain blue bodysuit," Keith said, handing her a large sandwich. "A lot of times people walk around in their big costume for only the hour before the costume contest, just for visibility. Other people really enjoy getting into character and don't mind."

Siona took a huge bite into the soft rye bread and corned beef. The delicious food almost made up for the hours she had spent inside the sweltering costume. But not quite.

"You should add a ventilation shaft and a small fan," she said. "I'm sure the wearer would appreciate airflow."

"That's a great idea," Kayla said. "I don't think I will have to incorporate that into the design this time, but it's something to think about. Why haven't I thought about that?"

"Probably because you have always been on the outside," Siona said drily. "If you were the one suffering to breathe, you would have figured it out much sooner."

"Oh, cousin you have no idea," Keith snorted from the corner. "Some of us will gladly suffer for our art. Some of these costumes take years to make and are only worn a few times a year."

Siona looked around at the costumes in the shop. They were magnificent and she couldn't deny the work and creativity that went into their construction. Her cousins obviously had talent and skill when it came to their creations. Nothing left their shop before it was perfect. Over the past few days, they had gone into overdrive. At least three dozen people had come in for final fittings and to pick up costumes. Siona had recognized very few of the characters, but the majority of them she had no idea about it.

"Something I don't understand about Cos-play," she said. "Why spend so much time, money, and energy on a costume? Why is there so much investment?"

Kayla looked at her and gave a small smile. Siona waited for her to finish her sandwich.

"Funny that you, of all people, should ask a question like that," her cousin said. "Being a stargazer and all."

"What do you mean? The stars are real, and people have been studying them for years," Siona said.

"And there have been many ideas about things that people can't even see. Yet, people like you, go ahead and create theories about what is up there and how it affects us. I find it amazing you can conceptualize galaxies that are millions of lightyears away, but are amazed that people get involved with imaginary worlds," Kayla said. "Cosplay is just another amazing way to immerse yourself into your favorite world. It's just another way to embrace something you love. I mean, haven't you ever read a book where you identified with the world and the people so much that you could imagine living there? This is just a more satisfying way to live it out."

Siona nodded, she did have her favorite works that had pulled her in deeply, but she still didn't quite get the whole comic book thing. However, she suspected part of that was because comic books meant thinking about Mathias. And she wasn't ready to cry again.

"Well once you are done with your food, I need to stand for about thirty more minutes so I can make sure the connectors are all good. Misty is coming by early in the morning to get it."

Siona nodded and took another large bite of her sandwich, figuring it would be a long day and she would need the energy.

One bright summer day after her twentieth year festivities, Vestele Fi-Volance goes for a walk to clear her head. At her party, her parents had announced her betrothal to a Prince of from the Kingdom of Fire, on the southern border of their lands. As she walks to contemplate her fate, a strange young man named Nidedric Sonis approached her and begs to talk to her. Nidedric claims Vestele was actually his sister, one who had been kidnapped at birth, but the information had been kept secret from him until recently. He only learned the truth because a trusted servant revealed it to him on her deathbed. He tells her a fantastic tale about how Vestele was taken to shift the balance of power from the Kingdom of Water, and delivered to the Kingdom of Air. He then produces a gemstone and claims that only a member of his family can make the stone shine with power. Vestele is curious about his story, but remained distrustful of the stranger. He pressed the stone into her hand and to her surprise; she hears the sound of the ocean.

Before the two can talk anymore, her handmaidens come looking for her, and when she looks around Nidedric is gone. Vestele can't stop thinking of the story, and begins to look around to see if she can find out any information.

She isn't even sure if he spoke the truth, but she still has the stone. Even more, late at night, after waking from one of her night terrors, she finds the stone in her hand, glowing with a blue light. Even more, she feels a slight flow of wind swirling over her hand that holds the stone.

Vestele decides that she will go in search of Nidedric and find out the truth for herself. Her adventure will take her through the lands of the other elemental elven kind. She will also have to figure out the truth of her situation. Did the only family she knows steal her, and if so why? Will she ever meet up with Nidedric? What will her travels ultimately reveal to and about her? This is the story of a young elven princess who has to decide if Fate or Duty is her true calling. All the while, deciding who is friend and who is foe, and learning more about herself than she could ever imagine. Each choice comes with a cost and a reward, but it is up to her to make the best calls.

Siona listened, transfixed, to the backstory about the character she was going to portray. As if being an amazing costume designer weren't enough, Keith was one heck of a story teller.

"What happens?" she asked. "Does she find out who she really is? And can she really make the choices?"

"I don't know," Keith said, holding a piece of fabric up next to her face.

She scoffed at him as he rapidly switched out swatches of fabric, until finding the shade of blue he was looking for.

"How can you not know? You're the one telling the story," she said.

"Vestele isn't a character I play. I know the basics of the story: all the adventures, the pitfalls, the challenges and even a good surprise or two, but what is played can be completely different. Depending on what is rolled and the choices the player makes, she could fall over a cliff and die bloody and alone, or fall over a waterfall and find out she commands the water," he said.

"What kind of crap is that?" Siona asked. "Seriously, you don't know what is going to happen to her?"

She sighed as Kayla and Keith shared an amused grin.

"Do you want to play it out?"

Siona stared at them.

"Play it out? You mean roll dice and act it out and such?"

Kayla and Keith laughed at her, for far too long.

"It wasn't that funny," she muttered.

"I'm going to run to the store and get the rest of the supplies before they close," Keith said standing. "I would prefer not to pull an all-nighter before our big presentation."

Siona looked in the mirror stunned. She wasn't sure if she should be horrified or thoroughly impressed. She couldn't quite believe her eyes, but there she was, dressed as an elven princess. The tunic was a shade of blue that fluxed between blue, a bluish-purple-aqua, and aqua. It wasn't as tight as she had expected, nor did her cleavage spill over the top. The leggings were ivory with rows of iridescent sequins down the sides. The wig she had on was plain brown but had a tiny crown sewn into the top. The best features of the crown were the small blinking lights Kayla had carefully wired. Siona didn't even mind the prosthetic ears glued on because it completed the look. Then there were the wings on her back. They were amazingly light, considering the LED lights that ran not only over the outside of the wings but also spiraled in a complex pattern to cover part.

"Are you sure I can't talk you into the contacts?" Keith said.

"But then I will have to stick my finger in my eye," she said.

"Yes," he rolled his eyes. "And it will complete the costume. No one will be able to recognize you."

"For the costume contest I will," Siona grumped after thinking hard about it. "If this is your one big chance at getting a break, I won't stand in the way."

She squeaked when Keith picked her up and twirled her around.

"Hey, now! Watch my wings, you idiots."

Siona laughed, a good cleansing laugh, as Kayla slapped at Keith's arms. She carefully made her way away from what was becoming an epic battle. Her cousins had grabbed unfinished foam swords and began swinging them at each other. Kayla clearly had more vigor and her brother yielded quickly. Everyone grinned, all the tension broken.

"Let's get you out of this costume," Kayla said. "We need to get these packed up and ready to go. For once we need an early bed time."

Siona took a deep breath. It was the last one she would have for the next two hours. She stood quiet while her cousins strapped her back into the costume. Kayla pulled the ribbons for the bustier tighter and Siona shot her a pained look in the mirror.

"I can't represent you well if I pass out."

"Nonsense, just make sure to flutter gently to the ground."

On top of the tunic and leggings she had tried on before, Siona wore a thin metallic breast plate and had wrist bands that hid smaller daggers. She had played around pretending to block bullets, until she got a glare. A few more tugs and pulls brought her back to her torture. Kayla reached under the tunic and clicked on the wings. They glowed and moved in slow sweeping motions. Her boots also glowed, and thankfully only had two inch heels.

"Now, get your ass over to make-up and go walk around a lot. The more people see you the better. Put a real smile on your face and stop for pictures if they ask. You are representing my dreams, don't mess fuck it up."

Siona would have told Keith about himself, but he had already moved on to the next model. She walked over to make-up, and sighed as she was handed the contact case. Forty-five minutes later and she was done. Looking in the mirror she gasped. She barely recognized herself. The purple contacts were awesome looking, but the make-up had completely changed her features. Her eyes looked wider but much more slanted. Her cheekbones were sharp and narrowed against her face. Her lips were plump and sparkled. Her skin was a light bronze and glittered as well.

"Go out and be Vestele-Fi," Kayla said.

For the next hour, Siona walked around. She was surprised at how many people wanted their picture taken with her. She dutifully handed out postcards with information about the game and her cousins costume shop. She also found it easy to get into character. It was fun not to be her for a while and since she had learned the backstory, she hammed it up.

Siona strutted down the catwalk. The costume contest was in full swing and she planned to win. As she landed at the end, she turned in a slow circle, pressing the control at her wrist that made her wings sweep grandly away from her, light up and small trails of steam poured from the top. The crowd cheered and hollered for her as she turned and walked away. As she waited backstage for the winners to be announced, she nervously held her cousins hands.

When their names were called, she walked out to accept the award. The cheering was thunderous and she grinned widely. She handed the plaque and envelope to her cousins, and then quietly walked away as designers swarmed her cousins. She decided it was okay to ruin her makeup and grab a snack. As she made her way through the curtains, she was asked to make the wings flow again. She smiled and complied. When she was done, she turned toward the food vendors and met a pair of familiar butterscotch eyes.

"Siona," he breathed.

"Hi Mathias."

Chapter 16

Mathias looked at the gorgeous woman standing before him and couldn't take a deep breath. The costume showed off her body to perfection. His hands itched to run over every curve and kiss his way up and down her body once again. The smile she gave him made his brain stutter.

Someone bumped into him as they stood staring at each other. He damn near growled as he realized that his eyes weren't the only ones on her. He knew she was waiting for a response to her greeting, but instead he watched other men pass by and check her out. He knew he needed to reach out soon.

"Siona."

As he breathed out her name, and felt his chest constrict as she not only looked at him but look through straight to his soul. He met her eyes again and time seemed to stop. Every fiber of his being hoped that she wouldn't reject him before he could explain everything to her. He waited for her to respond, a million of ways of begging for a second chance, waited on his lips.

"Hi Mathias."

Her soft voice stole his breath. He had missed her more than he had been willing to admit to himself. Not seeing her the past few days left an ache. Even Nathaniel had treaded carefully around him, and there had been a distinct lack of crass jokes. He alternated between wanting to thank Tess for her advice, and curse her for not giving him the magic words to make everything better. Instead he would have to fumble his way through.

"You look amazing. I was completely sold on your act up there for the costume contest. And by the way, I'm not at all surprised you won. Your cousins did a great job of transforming you into a whole other character," he said. "The make-up is fantastic, it completely transforms you. But I knew it was you, under there."

"How did you?" she asked. "I barely recognize myself."

Mathias wanted to make a glib comment about being able to sniff her out, or talk about her scent, but they weren't in that place anymore. He had ruined that by accusing her of actions she had never taken. Ones he knew she never would have taken. Fear had made him an idiot and it was time to fix his wrongs. He took a deep breath and smiled again at her. He wanted to pull her into his arms and kiss away the cautious look she gave him.

"I would know you anywhere. Can you possibly forgive me for having a freak out and behaving like a complete asshole?"

She blushed and dipped her head. The wings on her back slowly swished back and forth. The steam that pulsed from the top of the wings created a halo of fog around her, making her more ethereal looking. Mathias realized, in that moment, that he would tell her how he felt. She might tell him to suck rocks, but at least he would be honest with her. The silence lasted a bit too long and Siona looked around, nervous.

"I didn't expect to see you here," she said.

151

He saw her gaze land on her cousins, who were talking to a small gathering of people. She had every right not to want to talk to him. He wasn't safe for her anymore. Mathias took advantage of her safety net being occupied.

"I could give you some lame excuse, like this is the first annual Comic Convention that the University of Flint is hosting. As a comic book fan, I was practically obligated to show up," he said. "But the truth is that I knew you were going to be here and I wanted to see you before you left to go home."

The purple contacts in her eyes, made the gaze she gave him eerie. It was like they could see through him, into his very essence. She blinked slowly and he felt his heart hammer in his chest. The words spilled out of her mouth.

"If you came to make sure I wasn't going to say anything, you didn't need to bother. I spent the last few days being upset, crying even, and never uttered a single word about you to my cousins," she said. "Other than to call you a few choice words. And to wish you into positions that may or might not be possible considering your anatomy."

Mathias bit back a grimace because he could have sworn that she also tried hard to stay neutral in their conversation. She was mad and deserved to be so, but she had talked to him. It gave him some hope. He wanted their ease with each other back.

"I am pretty flexible, in one way or another," he teased gently.

Her laughter was loud and natural. It caught them both by surprised.

"So you're allowed to go there?"

He shrugged. Mathias knew what she asked for. She had no idea where he stood with her having the information.

"I am trying to let you know that I believe you. I know you wouldn't do anything to hurt us. Especially me. I've never been forced into a change. I was scared."

"I meant what I said before," Siona said, dropping into a lower and more serious tone. "You can have the damn rock. I won't ever say anything. It's not me. I like you."

"I know. I'm an asshole for even suggesting you would. You probably should have punched me in the mouth."

"Oh, I wanted to. At least twice," her head tilted to the side. "How did you know I was going to be here? I don't think you ever answered that question."

Mathis started to answer her, but a flurry of activity interrupted him. One minute he and Siona were having a fairly intimate conversation; the next they were surrounded by a small group of people including her cousins. He stepped out of the way, as they examined every aspect of her costume. He stifled the urge to throw his own punches as she was manhandled by a couple of guys.

"Chill out, lover boy, they want to know about how the costume works, not her body. They barely see her as a person in there. They're looking at my tech."

He looked up and met Kayla's brown eyes. Mathias was surprised at how much she resembled Siona. He'd never paid attention before. Same diamond face and even the same sprinkle of freckles over the cheeks. He had totally no reaction towards her though. Except profound gratitude.

"Do all costume designers feel up all their models?"

"Pretty much," Kayla grinned. "Jealous?"

"Of course I am. That man has his hands down her top in public and no one is saying anything because he is a designer. "

"Hell, why do you think I got interested in costuming in the first place?"

The second voice was lower and not quite as glib. Again the family resemblance struck Mathias. It was clear Kayla and Keith were twins, but Siona easily could have been their third. He stuck out his hand toward his cousin, and only had to wait an exaggerate pause before it was shook.

"You must be Keith."

"She wouldn't let me kick your ass, you know."

"She should have," Mathias said evenly. "It might have dislodged my head earlier."

He smiled at Keith threw his head back and laughed. Tension around them broke. Mathias winked at Siona as she tried to look at them, but couldn't. He watched the designers dissect each part of the costume, distracting her again. She was starting to look irritated.

"I can see why she likes you."

"Hopefully she remembers why she does too. I'm not sure I deserve the second chance that I want. Not to mention, she's leaving soon and I can't get back the time I wasted."

"She was broken up, man. You better be careful this time..."

Mathias received the threat loud and clear. Keith walked over to the group again, as Kayla waved him over. Watching Siona spin around in the costume, stole his attention again. He dug into the tight pockets of his costume and grabbed his phone. He unabashedly snapped photos of her as she modeled for the designers.

"Okay, we need to go speak with the designers again," Kayla said interrupting his photoshoot. "Can I trust her to your care?"

"Yes," he said. "Thanks."

She nodded and he smiled.

"By the way, if you want a real costume and not some plastic mesh glued on a sweatshirt, call us. I really should have found you a costume when you stopped by this morning. I'm kind

154

of embarrassed to let her be seen with you," Kayla said with distaste written all over her face. "The reboot sucked you know. Even the costumes were pitiful, and that is saying a lot considering the first remake. Hell, the very least you could have done is gone for the human fiery costume. Then again, you probably would have mangled that too. Take care with her feelings. I have a soldering iron."

"I got it. I owe you one," Mathias said.

"Yes, you do."

Earlier in the day, at the crack of dawn, he had gone to the shop hoping to find one her cousins. Kayla had been there, without coffee since Keith was out buying it. She glowered at him as he approached her and explained his side of the story. It had been easy to admit that he had been afraid of the building feeling he had for her cousin. It was much harder to hear about the tears he had caused Siona to shed.

"Why should I help you talk to her?" Kayla said. "You acted like a twelve year old. She is going home in a few days, just leave her in peace."

"Because we have a connection," he said, unknowingly, echoing Siona's word. "I messed it up, but I want to fix it before she leaves. I do care about her."

"I should trust you, why? Siona is my family."

"If you don't help me here, I will just go to New York and find her there. I came to you, because I being honest with my interest and intent. I know how much you mean to her. I'm trying to make up for being stupid."

Kayla grunted.

"You better have something good to say to her."

Fast forward a few hours and Mathias walked around the Con hoping to accidentally on purpose bump into Siona. He had gotten there when the event had opened and had had no luck. His wish was finally granted as the costume show began. When she walked down the stage, his heart stuttered. Even dressed up he knew her. He cheered the loudest when she had won. Then he waited patiently to get to talk to her.

"Do you want to grab a coffee?"

Siona's voice brought him back to the current moment.

"Done being felt up?" he joked.

"I hope not."

His breath stopped. Mathias took in a shaky breath. While he appreciated that she was joking with him, his mouth went dry at the thought of touching her again.

"How about that coffee?" his voice cracked as he asked. Mathias held both her hands and stared into her hazel eyes. "I am sorry. I insulted you and your integrity. I know you wouldn't have said anything. I know you are damn good person. And yes, in two weeks I have managed to connect to you more than I ever thought possible."

The words rushed out before he realized his own intentions. Siona leaned in and kissed him on the cheek.

"It took the advice of a friend to help me see the truth. I almost let my own stupid fears ruin what we had. I know I was a dick and pushed it on to you. It had nothing to do with the other night. I had neither reason nor right to treat you like that. I didn't want to admit that I didn't want our time to end," Mathias said. "I want more and I am willing to make it work."

"Thanks."

"I'm serious Siona. Even after you go home, I don't want us to end."

"Neither do I."

"Let's go talk about it."

They walked a few paces and after a quiet pause she stopped and just stared at him. Her eyes crinkled and she bit her bottom lip. He watched her swallow her laughter.

"I have to know, what are you wearing?"

"I'm the guy from the movie the other night. The one we saw at the drive-in."

"Which movie? No one was wearing sweats with odd pieces of garbage glued to them," she said.

"The torch?"

The giggles started out softly but turned into full blown laughter, complete with a snort.

"Wow, you really need to stick to star parties," Siona laughed. "That is possibly the worst costume I have seen here today."

"Only because you have been exposed to professional designs all week, and clearly I am not a costumer. Your cousin said the same thing, by the way. She offered to make me something less embarrassing. She also was the one who told me that you would be here today," he said, not at all afraid to admit he'd had help. "And I quote 'She will be at the convention. If you really have some kind of connection with her, you'll be able find her.' And I did, so here we are."

They finally made it over to where the food vendors had set up. They stood in line and Mathias winked at her. She winked back and it took a few moments for his brain to restart.

"I am glad I came here," he said.

"I am glad you did too," she said. "Although, it wouldn't hurt for you to tell me why."

"First, I got to see you dressed up like this. Second, you leave tomorrow. New York City is much bigger than Flint. It would've made it a bit harder to find you. Though I had a game plan, I knew where you worked."

"You would've had to get through security. They're kind of strict about research rights."

"I had a plan for that too," he said.

"Oh? And what would that be?"

"My secret," he said. "I made sure to have a back-up of my back-up where you were concerned."

Siona leaned in and kissed him. He took control and poured his emotions into their embrace. When they broke, he took her hand in his. He didn't plan to let he go until he absolutely had to.

"Do you have any other plans for today?" he asked.

"Just to get out of this costume," Siona said casually and then caught his eyes in hers. "Do you want to help?"

"I'm so glad you asked," he said. "Do you think the wings will fit in my car?"

Chapter 17

Siona rolled over and bumped into a large warm someone. She cautiously opened one eye, and then with a grin, snuggled into Mathias's back.

"Any chance I can get you to model that Princess-Ninja outfit for me again?"

The sleepy question made her laugh.

"No way. It took a ridiculous amount of time to get into it. And she is an elemental elf."

"But I was extra careful getting you out of it," he said. "You really rocked those wings."

She was pulled on top of him into an embrace. Siona looked down and leaned down to kiss him. Her stomach tightened deliciously as she responded to touching him. Pressing up to take a deep breath, she looked down at him in mock seriousness.

"Is it too soon to make dog breath jokes?" Siona asked.

Her question stopped his warm fingers from dancing up her spine in a gentle caress, and they drifted her sides. Her legs were trapped in his and he tickled her mercilessly. Siona never thought she would squeal, but she through her laughter and squirming.

"I'm sorry, it was wrong," she gasped. "But you laughed about it."

Once the tickling ceased she leaned down and began to nibble his lips. She pressed her lips firmly against his and slowly slid her tongue against his with slow sure swipes. His hands were warm and soft against the small of her back, holding her close. Her phone buzzed loudly and then heavy breathing and an ominous sounding ringtone began to play. Mathias began to chuckle.

"What? It's still a star based ring tone," she proudly defended her choice.

"Your job?"

"It's my dad," she said. "And before you ask, we have a great relationship."

The phone rang a few more times.

"Are you going to answer it?" he asked.

"Do you want to come meet my parents?" Siona rushed out and then blushed crimson. "Oh crap, it's too soon, isn't it? We've barely made peace, and then I... You know what? Never mind."

"I would love to meet your parents," Mathias said.

"You would?"
"Why not? I'm pretty fond of their daughter," he said.

Siona squinted her eyes and stared into his. She loved how the color was warm and her melt. She second guessed whether she should rescind the offer or not.

"Well, let's get dressed then," she said. "We are meeting for lunch before my flight."

She took a deep breath and prayed she wasn't making a huge mistake. Then she met Mathias eyes again and all the worry melted away.

Ten minutes later, hand in hand, Siona and Mathias walked through the doors of the diner.

"Mom, Dad. This is Mathias."

Siona stood from her desk with a stretch. It had been a long night of research and her bleary eyes reminded her that she had stared far too long at the computer screen. She organized her hastily scrawled notes and cleaned off her desk. She walked the long underground corridor with unhurried steps. It was the night after a full moon and Mathias probably wouldn't be calling until nine. She grinned as she realized she actually enjoyed his wolf nature. It still fascinated her, but she knew she had plenty of time to learn more about it.

She thought about walking the few extra blocks to get breakfast because plenty of time to get home. It would be the perfect way to pass the time rather than driving herself crazy by spending the next hour staring at her phone. Siona grinned, thinking about the surprise she had in plan for him. She hoped he would be just as excited as she was. The phone rang, startling her into fumbling and accidentally answering it. She recovered by leaning against the wall, as if she meant to do it on purpose—even though no one was around to see her. She put a purr into her voice.

"Hey, sexy man. I wasn't expecting to hear from you for a little bit. How are you this morning? Did you dream about me?"

"This is Mom. Sorry to let you down. Didn't you even look at the phone display?"
Siona looked down at her phone in surprise. She had never been so

glad to have an office all to herself. She could feel the heat pour into her cheeks.

"Umm, hi Mom," she said. "No. I didn't look at the display. I was kind of daydreaming and the phone startled me."

"I always call at eight," her mother said drily. "Mathias calls at six, what changed for today?"

Oh nothing, he went on his monthly run as a werewolf. Siona thought in total snark.

"He had a late night program, so we planned for a later call," Siona said.

"And apparently some phone sex to go with it."

She felt her entire ace flame, even though no one was around to see her. Siona knew her mother never pulled punches, but sometimes she did wish that her mother was less intuitive. She cleared her throat to ask what her mother needed, when she was interrupted.

"We need to talk."

"Why does this sound so ominous? It's too early in the morning for end of the world news, Mom," Siona said in a dry tone.

"Okay," her mother conceded. "Let me try again."

Siona rolled her eyes at the various vocal warm ups her mother went through. A few last minute coughs sounded real and made her wonder what really was about to be said.

"Good morning, Si," her mother said in a bright and cheery tone.

"Good morning, mother," she replied.

"Dad and I have decided to move back to Michigan," her mother said with no warm up. "With no family here and use being retired, we have opted to be closer to the family we have left."

"What? Mom, you can't just spring something like that on me," she exclaimed. "And what do you mean no family? I am here."

"Of course darling, but you have met the mob of family we have back in Michigan," her mother said, her voice still cheery. "You, darling daughter, are grown and out of the house. You have your own life and are busy. Dad and I are retired. His parents have been gone a while now, and I'm ready to go home."

There was a tone of finality in her mother's voice.

"Wow. I sure didn't see this coming," Siona said. "I guess I should come over for dinner tonight? Find out the finer details?"

"That sounds good; you can help us start to pack."

"Pack? Why are you packing?"

"Because we are moving," her mother said patiently. "We talked to an agent, and she said she had at least three clients who could potentially make an offer on our place by the end of the week. In addition, the agent in Michigan called, and there are homes for us to see out there as well. Dad and I plan to fly out there this weekend."

"I should have stuck with the ominous sounding warning," Siona said. "At least that would have prepared me for what was going to be said."

She frowned at the sound of her mother's laughter.

"Love you daughter. See you tonight," her mother said and hung up.

Siona sat stunned, not sure what to think about her mother's announcement. She locked her lab and walked toward the exit. Her head fog was interrupted by sounds of cooing and squealing further down the hallways. Loud chipper voices alerted her to trouble ahead. Before she could turn around and take the long way around, Tony from HR, called out to her.

"Siona, come and see Lisa's baby before you leave for the day."

She gave a deep sigh and walked toward the group. Siona liked Lisa. The baby was what scared her. They were just tiny, fragile, beings and Siona feared she might break it. As she got closer, she could see the joy and pride on Lisa's face. She took her cowardly position at the outside of the small crowd and peeped over Tony's shoulder to see. She saw a round face, with wide open eyes, and a mouth trying to envelop a plump fist.

"She is beautiful," Siona said.

"Do you want to hold her?" Lisa asked.

"I…ah… no thank you," she muttered.

She knew she was blushing and refused to make eye contact with any of the other women standing around. She appreciated the new mother didn't try to deposit the infant into her arms.

"Well thank you for your gift," Lisa said with an understanding smile. "You will be happy to know, her father and I decided to wait and use it to get her a telescope."

"That's awesome," Siona said. "It sounds like the perfect present to me."

She looked again at the small wriggling bundle, gave a quick smile to her mother and then began to walk out. She moved quickly with purpose toward the exit. The halls were clear and her escape seemed sure. Then a dark figure stepped into her line of sight and her heart sunk just a bit. She had no idea with the HR director would be intercepting her.

"Siona?" Kim called out to her.

"Yes?"

"Can I speak with you for a moment?"

She walked into the HR office and looked at the director.

"What's up?" she asked. "Did you finally decide that you are going to cut me into your winning pot?"

"Don't be silly," she said with a grin. "I am, however, going to give you a free day off."

"What? Why?" she asked, not sure if she should be thrilled to have another day off or if she should be concerned at her seeming generosity. "I already have three days off with my schedule."

"You look like you need another one this week. You have been working hard since you returned from the great mid-West. Now go and I will see you on Friday."

Siona pushed the door open, still slightly confused by Kim's — generosity and chose to walk home. The city was bustling as people made their way to work. She slowly walked down the steps and began the quarter mile trek, but stopped short.

"Mathias?" she gasped.

She hoped she wasn't hallucinating and was quickly reassured when he picked her up and hugged her.

"You didn't call me this morning," she said.

"I figured showing up would be better," he said as her gave her a soft kiss.

"What are you doing here?"

"Well, I heard about this really amazing planetarium with a research department to die for," he said. "Besides, it has been a whole two weeks since I have seen you."

Siona knew she was grinning like an idiot, but couldn't help herself.

"It certainly has been a long two weeks," she agreed.

"I know this is the end of your day, so I planned to take in a few shows while you sleep," he said.

Siona leaned in and kissed him. She felt herself slide down his body, reveling in his touch. Her mouth devoured his as she reacquainted herself with him. When they finally paused, all thoughts of walking home vanished.

"I have a better idea than sleep," she said and then grabbed his hand. "Taxi!"

Siona controlled herself admirably the whole ride back to her home. She paid the fare and then led him into the apartment building.

"It feels like we just drove around the block," Mathias said.

"It's about a quarter of a mile walk," Siona said. "I wanted to get home faster."

She felt her stomach clench at the smile he gave her.

"We're going to have some stairs to walk. The elevator is too rickety for my tastes," she said, opening the door to the stairwell.

"It's okay, I hate elevators anyhow," Mathias said.

Siona pulled him into another kiss, running her hands over his chest. She grumbled when he pulled away.

"I do not plan to make love to you in this foyer," Mathias said. "Let's go up to your place."

They made their way up the stairs, but the pace was leisurely as Siona took each floor landing as an excuse to kiss him. As she fumbled with the keys she looked up when he chuckled. For a moment their eyes met and after Mathias gave her a wink that revved her imagination, Siona dropped her keys. She managed to open the door and every inhibition of making out in public dropped.

"Just so you know, I plan to take you to bed and have my way with you," she gasped as his lips found a sensitive spot under her chin.

"Great," Mathias said. "Why did you tell me the obvious?"

"We said that open communication was the best," she said with a grin. "I don't want you to think that I lost my mind in a frenzy of passion. I figured that full disclosure would help you stay tethered to this plane of existence."

"How long have you been working on that line?" Mathias chuckled.

"About two weeks," she grinned.

They made it into her apartment in short order. As soon as the door shut, Siona began tugging at his shirt.

"You weren't kidding, were you?" he asked.

"Not at all. I have missed you," she said.

She tugged his hand and led him to her bedroom. She unzipped her pants and pulled them down. A momentary panic crossed her mind when Mathias gave her a curious look. Siona looked down and then back at him in confusion.

"What was that look for?"

"You like cotton panties. Cotton breathes, remember? Why the pink silk?"

She swallowed the embarrassment and gave him a knowing smile.

"Well, my plans for today included calling you after I got home. And then flirting with you by describing what I was wearing," she said, and unbuttoned her top to reveal a matching bra. "There were going to be some *movements* to go with the narration. You know, like jazz hands, but sexier."

Siona smiled as Mathias sucked in a hasty breath.

"You are the world's best girlfriend," he said.

"I know," Siona said. "However, since you are here, I think a change in plans is in order. Maybe I can instruct you how to use your hands on me?"

She watched his eyes slowly roam over her body.

"Okay."

"Well first you are going to finish unbuttoning my shirt, but don't touch anything but those buttons."

The heat from his hands scorched her skin, even though he carefully obeyed her orders.

"Second, I suggest we go into the bedroom, and you figure out the best way to remove the rest of my garments, using two fingers only."

She took Mathias's offered hand and followed him into her room. As his warm hands skimmed her skin again, she moved closer and began to feel heat pool in her stomach. She watched as his fingers skimmed over her breasts and teased her skin by dipping just under the lace of her bra.

"Now I would like for you to get totally naked and then sit in that chair," Siona said. "And then I plan to join you."

She gave Mathias a slow wink with a husky laugh.

"Let me welcome you to New York," she said, straddling his lap. "You can see the city later."

Chapter 18

Mathias woke up and curled around Siona. He watched her as she slept. Her breathing was soft and even. He nuzzled the back of her neck and was rewarded as she woke up and turned over. Her smile melted his heart and he kissed the tip of her nose.

"Hi," he said.

"Good evening," she grinned. "I'm starving. How do you feel about dinner?"

"I need some kind of food after your welcome. Not that I'm complaining because you're amazing."

She winked, leaned in to kiss him and climbed out of bed and walked to the bathroom. He reveled in the brief touch and felt like he'd been given a second chance. Mathias knew he'd been playing it safe for a long while. The whole event with Ebony had provided the perfect excuse for him to tap out of the dating scene. One he hadn't wanted to join anyhow, if he was completely honest.

He'd had his plate with being a werewolf, but he couldn't be a football player and not have a girlfriend. Being jilted by a woman for his brother made it easy for other guys to believe his pain, so there was no teasing or name calling.

Mathias sat up as she walked back into the room. She had the same expression as before when he had surprised her earlier. He would never forget how their eyes met and how he'd had kissed her as if his life depended on it, wanting nothing but to melt into her. He stared at Siona, waiting for any movement, the slightest indication she'd welcome his touch again. Her breath hitched once, twice, and then he was staring at her back as she turned and walked toward the closet.

"I'm going to be strong for both of us. Because if we make love again, one of us will pass out from malnutrition," she laughed. "I'll cook."

Mathias promised himself he would play by her rules. Even though it was the hardest thing he ever had to do. He hadn't kissed her in weeks and he was hungering for the taste of her, again. He walked over and kissed her on the shoulder before going to take a quick shower.

Once done, he dressed and then went to find her in her kitchen. He touched her as much as he could, brief little hand brushes as she made grilled cheese sandwiches. She didn't even seem to mind when his hands drifted down to her waist.

Mathias wanted to pull her closer and get full body contact, but knew she would pull away. She clearly was sticking to her food eating plan. He actually did want to see the city, he'd never been to New York, but staying in bed with her all night sounded good too. She'd already promised to give him a tour.

"Tomorrow's Sunday."

Siona looked up from the griddle and over her shoulder to meet his eyes. "That's generally the day that comes after Saturday."

Mathias rolled his eyes. He gently turned her around to face him and kissed her forehead.

"What I mean is that we have a long weekend. So I was thinking maybe we can fix a problem?"

She tilted her head as she regarded him thoughtfully. "What problem? What did you have in mind?"

Mathias hoped his voice stayed casual.

"I thought we could go to the Custer Institute and have a look at their dark sky park. We could have a date do over."

He hoped his idea would be met with enthusiasm. After the debacle at the park in Michigan, he felt they were owed a good date. They both loved the skies and to have the tainted memories as their only reminder seemed wrong to him. They needed a star date and fortunately, New York also had a dark sky park. Mathias doubted Siona had even thought of going, but he knew it would be instrumental to them starting over with a clean slate.

And if a ruling Deity was somewhere listening, he would be able to cuddle with her under the skies and kiss her senseless. And once he started again, nothing was going to make him stop. Siona seemed to take forever in answering and the anticipation made him rethink his idea. Maybe she thought it was stupid or a bad idea and didn't know how to tell him. He froze for a few moments while she thought it over, and remembered to breathe again when her face lit up.

"Sounds fun. I think it's a good idea to make some new memories. Not to mention, I've never actually been. Pitiful since I live here, but true nonetheless. Are you sure you want to go?"

"Yes. Our plans got a bit derailed last time."

She nodded as she turned around to flip the sandwiches over.

"Do you want one or two?"

"Three please. The park is only about an hour and a half away. How have you never been there?"

"No car," she reminded him.

"Oh the pain of choosing your scope over a car."

Siona laughed as she grabbed more bread. Mathias knew he would spend all day watching her, if he could. He recalled Tess saying he was smitten, and he wholeheartedly agreed. He wasn't sure how the whole long distance relationship thing would work out, but he wasn't going to let her slip through his fingers.

"Dinner," she proclaimed.

"It looks great," he said.

"It does, if I say so myself."

Mathias pulled her into a kiss before following her into the living room to eat. They ate in comfortable silence, until Siona's yawns broke in.

"How about we watch a movie and stay in tonight?" he suggested. "We're going to be up late tomorrow night and you're already off schedule from today."

"And staying home tonight seems to be the best option for extra rest?"

"You don't think so?"

"I don't know that we'll sleep."

"I promise to behave," he said with a grin.

"Hold on a minute, I didn't say it was a bad idea. I was merely making an observation. And just because you plan to behave doesn't mean I do."

He stared at her, all words left his head. She winked and smiled at him.

"Fine. I'll behave."

"Then come on woman, the couch is calling our name and there are movie choices to scroll through."

Mathias walked over and tugged her towards the living room. Giggling, she resisted, pulling back. A confused look crossed over his face until she burst into laughter and said, "Let me make some popcorn first. Who watches a movie without?"

He nodded and walked into the living room. He smelled the popcorn, and despite having just eaten, was hungry again. When she headed towards him from the kitchen, he could hear her catch her breath at the hungry look written all over his face. One that had nothing to do with popcorn.

He smiled and reminded himself they were just going to watch a movie. Even after spending the better part of the afternoon in bed, he wanted to caress and cuddle with her. He planned to watch a movie and assured himself that nothing else was going to happen. Mathias grabbed Siona's hand again and pulled her onto the sofa, but was careful to make sure none of the popcorn spilled. Mathias kept her hand, entwining their fingers.

If someone asked him what the movie was, he never would have been able to tell them. She had chosen some action packed flick, but it didn't hold his attention at all. Instead he watched her. He tried to memorize every smile, jump, and laugh for later when he was back home without her.

He stayed true to his words and continued to keep his hands to himself, but he did his best to allow her to enjoy the movie. Mathias knew Siona's sexual appetite matched his, but it wasn't just a physical act for him. He had had plenty of time to think about why he was alone and had come to the conclusion that he wasn't willing to just be with anyone. If he was going to forge a relationship with someone, it would be long term. Otherwise, why bother? He made the decision to be open and honest with her.

They sat in silence, just enjoying the chatter from the movie and the presence of the other. As soon as the film ended he broke the silent promise to himself and leaned over and kissed her. When Siona tried to move him along, Mathias refused to relinquish her hand, leading her back into her bedroom. He sat her down on the edge of the bed before he began stripping off his clothes. Siona opened her mouth once to protest and then closed it again when he held up his hand. He could see the questioning in her eyes.

There was a slight chill due the air conditioning, but Mathias wasn't cold as Siona's eyes practically devoured him. The members of the Pack learned to be comfortable nude, but Siona made him very aware of his body. The looks she gave him gave his imagination clear reign on what she could be thinking. His own, obliging brain provided images of Siona naked and willing to explore with him. To his alarm, he felt his body beginning to respond to those fantasies. He'd actually had a reason for being naked in front of her, and they had nothing to do with sex.

"This is from the first time I changed. I had no idea what happened and spent a lot of time running through the woods. I barely remember getting it."

He pointed to a jagged line, barely visible against his ribcage.

"We heal quickly, but this was deep and got infected because my allergy to poison ivy. It gave me tangible proof that I hadn't been dreaming."

He smiled as Siona sat up taller on the edge of the bed where he'd left her. He turned and pointed to faded marks on his hip.

"The day Nathaniel and I became friends, I punched him in the face for making fun of my solar system project. A few years later, he tried to mock in front of the pack. I beat him down again and told him to bite my ass. He took me literally."

Mathias grinned as she laughed out loud. He carefully went each and every mark he'd gotten being a werewolf.

"I made some unfair accusations toward you," he said and then held up his hand again to stop her protest. "I don't want you to give me the out of being scared about being forced to change in front of you. I reacted out of fear because I was already in love with you by then."

He wasn't ready for her quick rise to her feet. Her mouth crushed against his and he enjoyed the silky feel of her lips. Mathias, regretfully, led her back to the bed.

"I need to finish, and you, my beautiful distraction, have to let me. As I said, I had no fear that you would betray us. I didn't know how to be in love with you and deal with the fact that you were leaving."

"You love me? So I'm not the only one…"

Mathias leaned in kissed her last words away. She had given him a glimmer of hope that he wasn't in it by himself. As they stared at each other after their outpouring, Mathias backed up, and took a few tentative steps towards Siona, again. He needed to get the rest out.

"Before you, I only dated a woman one time. Not a single one had ever attracted me like you did. I didn't know what to do with my feelings."

He liked how she met his eyes without hesitation. His heart pounded as he fell into her gaze and felt like the air was charged. Mathias turned away to slip back into his clothes. When he looked back, he found her staring. As he watched, her gaze traveled across his body, seeing and memorizing each mark he'd pointed out like it was a map to his soul.

Mathias swallowed nervously against a dry mouth, waiting for her to finish. When she looked up at him, his eyes dropped to her mouth. He could feel the heat exuding off of her as she stood up and stepped in close. Then the pull between them intensified and drowned out everything else.

She took one more step closer, then a second, and then he reached out to touch her. Mathias ran his fingertips down her cheek and Siona's eyes half-closed in reaction to the gentle touch. His hand curved around her neck and brushing his thumb against her jawbone, he leaned down towards her and their lips met. The kiss started gentle at first, but then turned fierce, passionate and consuming. Siona's arms came up around Mathias's neck, her fingers snaking through his hair as she melted into him. Mathias growled once, low in his throat, using his other arm to anchor her tightly against his body.

Time warped around them and all he knew was Siona and how she made him feel. He nuzzled her neck and had the pleasure of hearing her heart skip a beat when he nipped her. The last bit of fear about risking his heart with her fell away.

"I've never had a relationship, let alone a long distance one. However, I'm willing to try," he said. "I'll probably mess it up a lot. But I'll never stop trying to make it work with you."

Nothing could have prepared him for the tears mixed with laughter and babbling. He couldn't understand a word she said, but knew it was all good.

"You're going to have to translate for me," he chuckled.

"I said, I want to work on it with you too."

When Mathias woke the next morning, his euphoric mood hadn't worn off, and he couldn't wait for them to spend time at the Dark Sky Park. He lay next to her listening to her breathe and relaxed. He could easily imagine waking next to her every morning.

After a sensual start to their day, he and Siona visited her favorite diner and spent the day in the planetarium. Mathias couldn't help the giddy feeling, even though the Longway had the better equipment. Siona convinced him to let her go as a tourist with him and promised a behind the scenes tour later.

They rented a car and at dusk made their way out to the Custer Institute and Observatory gem on Long Island. It was nestled in a small house with a tiny dome. They missed the quiet road and had to turn around twice, while finding it. The weather gods had listened and they were treated to a clear, cloudless sky.

Even though, Siona had brought her own equipment, the dome had a 25" telescope which they spent equal amount of time looking through. Mathias and Siona played it up and "oohed" and "ahhhed" at the impressive look at stars, double binaries, nebulae, star clusters, planets, and the moon.

"Let's go outside."

He didn't need Siona to ask twice, and with the volunteers help, made their way back toward the dark field behind the main building. A handful of other people walked around, using giant binoculars and personal telescopes, talking in hushed tones.

While she looked through the scope, questions began circling around in his head.

What would his pack think about him dating her? Never mind what the others thought, what did she think? When she said she wanted to be with him, how much? His mind briefly flashed to the previous nights, of the heated kisses they shared, which still made him feel liquid warmth inside. If she hadn't been on vacation would she have thrown caution to the wind? This thing between Siona and him had only just heated up over the last few weeks, just in time for the debacle. He didn't think it too soon for anything really serious, or was he just fooling himself?

While Siona peered into the eyepiece of her scope, oblivious to his preoccupied daze, Mathias made a decision. He would start moving forward and make it clear exactly where his intentions lay. By the time they made it back to her apartment, he had it all planned. He'd wait for Siona to get out of the shower, maybe even kiss up and down her good morning. He'd touch her any chance he got, laying his scent on her skin. He could hardly wait.

The next morning Mathias made breakfast and waited for her to get out of the bathroom, having decided to go for broke. He had a few things to put in place, and then he was going to make his claim perfectly clear.

"What's all this?" she asked.

"Breakfast," he said with a shrug. "I only have another day with you, so I plan to spoil you as much as I can."

He loved the way the blush covered the curve of her cheek.

"You know you can't spoil me, and then leave, right?"

"I'll just give you something to hold on to, until the next visit."

Mathias grabbed her hand and led her back to bed.

178

Chapter 19

Mathias sat at his desk getting ready to rowdy group of students coming in to explore all periods, not just the Jurassic, with the Dinosaurs and Fossils class. It was the last summer class they were hosting and he was glad. Even though he knew sand and dirt were part of the excitement, he still didn't know the kids managed to spread it so far outside the classrooms. His phone chimed.

I wish you were here.

He could hear the longing and excitement from her text. He responded with a grin. It grew wider and he rolled his eyes at himself for being so giddy about a text from her.

Where? Not at the conference, but which seminar did you go to? Will I be jealous?

Of course he knew he would be jealous. After weeks of researching programs, Siona had found out about a conference in New Jersey covering not only new topics in astrophysics and would feature quite a few notable names in scholarly programs that she was interested in.

I'm listening to a talk about On the Role Particle Drifts in the Heliosphere. I'm hoping to meet up with a few faculty members from some of the different programs. But the real reason for my text is because I found out we're hosting a series of seminars at the Hayden in November. All that to say— I know when and where our next visit will be. I'll chat with you later.

Mathias could feel the infectious joy coming from her and, not for the first time, was a bit bummed that he couldn't have joined her at the conference. His phone buzzed and when he checked, he was rewarded with a selfie from her.

He smiled as he thought about his visit to New York. Despite the steamy start, and the Dark Sky Park, Siona made good on her promise and did show him around the city. For his last two days there, they had played the ultimate tourists and visited the Statue of Liberty, the Empire State Building, and even Times Square. He laughed about eating their way through most of the rest of the city, including what seemed to be every food truck they saw. His visit got even more interesting when they tried to have a picnic in Central Park.

Siona had been so excited to surprise him; she kept the plans for the day a huge secret. They started off with the private tour of the Hayden she had promised, in the research department. She had even proudly showed him off to her co-workers. He gave Tony a big thank-you for helping set up her time off for his visit and then went on to be impressed by the scope of her work. Mathias caught a particular scent when walking out of the American Museum of Natural History toward their destination. He grabbed her hand and pulled her to face him.

"Where are we going?" he had asked.

"I have a picnic set up for us," she had smiled. "I have a basket and everything waiting. I had to pay the carousel guy a premium to hold it for me."

"Siona, I think we need to make other plans for our picnic," he had said.

"Why?"

"The park isn't a good fit for me, not quite my taste," he said.

"Mathias, just try it. I promise the picnic will be fun. We will avoid sitting on ant hills."

He met her bemused look and tried to explain again.

"It's kind of full."

"What are you talking about?" she had asked. "It's the middle of the day, on a Thursday. There is plenty of room. We will probably be the only tourists there."

"I'm pretty certain I won't be welcome," Mathias pressed.

"Why not? Everyone is welcome, it's a public park."

"I'm sure every *person* is welcome there, but I doubt my kind is," he stressed.

He wanted to laugh at how round Siona's eyes got. She had leaned her head in close.

"You mean to tell that Central Park has a...*a pack*?" she whispered.

"Yeah. And I have no desire to find out whether or not they want me there or not. Let's find another place to have a picnic. I would like my vacation to remain confrontation free."

"Where do you want to go? I can't think of anywhere else good. Oh wait, we could go to Coney Island."

"And get a real Coney dog?"

"Weren't you the one to tell me they started in Michigan? This is an adventure park."

"We haven't had enough adventure? Although, evading a run in with other werewolves does count. There aren't any at Coney Island are there?"

She had laughed and kissed him; then loftily informed him.

"You never know, it's located at Luna Park. Though, with all the people already there, we might not even know the difference. And if they are there, I will defend you."

They had laughed between kisses. All the activities and fun kept them busy, until they returned to her place. The next day had been spent re-exploring each other until hunger drove them out of bed. In between bites of takeout food, Siona had filled him in on her plans to look for a new school to start her advanced degree. Mathias found himself getting just as excited as she. In the end, she figured she might as well stay in New York and continue her degree in the program she had loved. He smiled as he recalled his vacation; it had been an amazing visit.

"Do you have a second to talk about *Poetry Under the Stars?*"

He looked up as his jaunt down memory lane was interrupted and smiled at Dina, his assistant. She had coordinated the newly established, but very popular poetry and yoga programs. They had been so wildly successful that the waiting lists had waiting lists, so he wasn't surprised she wanted to talk. She sat down and outlined her new plans for expansion. The next twenty minutes passed quickly as she detailed the new schedule.

"You're making me look good," he said.

"I know right?" she laughed back. "I should get a raise, right?"

"You are right, so you just go ahead and talk to Todd about that. He might consider it since Mel is leaving. Of course, he might also want you to dip your toes into the kiddie pool. More and more parents are trying to make their children fall into the "indigo" category everyone is chatting about lately."

Her comeback was cut off as the sound of twenty kindergarten children filled the halls. Mathias wanted to point out how quickly her face grew pale at the noise, but she grinned and stood up.

"I am so glad that I work with the grown variety," Dina said. "Your public waits. Have a great time with the little spawn."

"What you're really saying is "Mathias, I would love the opportunity to work with five year olds'," he said. "You know, you could take over Mel's position."

"Your obvious lack of sex is obviously making you hear things that make no sense," she scoffed. "We both know you don't want me to interact with the little …darlings. I mean, they would run around shrieking and ask about dinosaurs, and then I would tell them about the act of reproduction. Soon the talk would digress into how T-Rex's aren't good at the sexy time because their arms are too short to spank during the good parts, and it would just get bad after that."

"There it is; the reason people think all new-agey, metaphysical people are in it for the orgies. And this is why I let you arrange classes in yoga and poetry; for adults," he laughed. "You are the perfect guide to help repressed souls find enlightenment. Now, if you will excuse me, I have some children to educate. Properly."

"Go ahead Boss-Man," she called to him. "But I bet you won't get that visual out of your head for anything."

Mathias chuckled as he walked toward the classroom and the cacophony of excitement. He had the perfect counter visual to concentrate on.

Later that night Mathias pushed paws into the soft mud, glad his lupine face wouldn't grimace. Ever since his second grade Halloween party and the guts bowl, he hated the feel. Even in wolf form he still hated the slimy feeling on his wrists. He also knew that his packmates would spare no expense to mock him, if they ever found out. The run was timely. After a week full of children's programs, in which he had been the primary teacher, he needed the stress release. The children not only tried to break every piece of equipment his grant had lovingly provided, but whined about it the entire time. He had broken away from the group, and took advantage of the run.

Why can't I use the big telescope? Why aren't we allowed to ride the rollercoaster forever? Why do we have to watch the baby show? Why is this show so boring? I thought we were going to make real rockets, this is stupid. Don't we get a snack? My momma thought you would feed us; the other program has free lunch.

His thoughts ran over what his schedule held for the next week. Mathias realized he would need to drink, a lot. Someday he would tell Granny he went back on his promise, just after he made her run a program with the little deviants. In that moment he also realized how much he needed to replace his colleague.

He ran faster, avoiding brambles and braches, desperately trying to clear his mind. There was a lot to finish up and very little time to do it in. He still needed to finalize the plans for the Great Lakes Planetarium Association's conference the Longway was hosting in October. His second thought had been to fly out and join Siona at the next Astrology conference. He actually had voiced the idea to Nathaniel, and endured almost five full minutes of laughter.

"Your plan is to go meet up with your woman—at a conference— about stars—and you plan to get laid?" Nathaniel had gasped out. "You do realize that you two nerds will spend all of your time listening to other space nerds talk about theories, right? What a stupid plan."

He shook his head at his friend's crass advice. Nathaniel might be an overly loud jerk, but it didn't mean he wasn't right. It also didn't mean Mathias didn't take pride in wanting to be with Siona at a scholarly convention. He enjoyed the fact they could talk shop and find it stimulating. Maybe the feeling was just the newness of finding a person that you connected with completely, but he didn't care. He wanted to have as much time with her as possible.

To his surprise caught a scent of a deer, even though his thoughts kept rambling. He looked around and didn't see anyone else. While he had been up in his head, he'd wandered off on his own. Mathias had never really gone after any of the hunt animals. He always joined the chase with his friends, but had zero desire to take one down himself. Tonight was different.

It's about time I finally gave in. I found a girl and she found out the truth. Aside from being a little too excited about it, she's still into me. I think it's time I get just as excited about being me.

He flattened himself closer to the ground and moved faster to intercept his prey. He held himself still and waited for the right moment. Mathias saw it eating from a bush. It was young and inexperienced, but still wary. Its head bobbed up and down as it ate. Every once in a while it would look around for danger. But the tail was down, meaning it really wasn't on alert.

Mathias slunk closer, and attacked. The deer scrambled toward the tree line and out of sight, but it didn't matter. He already had the scent in his nose. He ran harder on this chase than any other before. His thoughts tumbled through his brain, trying to make sense of what he really wanted for his life. The doubled back in front of him and he leapt.

His jaws snapped close on its neck and he dragged his prey toward the ground. He heard and then felt the others come to his aid. They worked as a flawless team and the kill was made. Mathias looked at his packmates, his friends, and knew the talk he would be having soon. But for tonight, he planned to enjoy the party.

Mathias paced back and forth. He waited for his boss to come in to ask him for a favor. All the pieces of his plan were falling into place. He had talked to Marcus, as well as his friends. It took a moment to get everyone on board, but they had come around. Their blessings were given and he was ready for the final piece.

"Mathias, can you come up front, please?"

The intercom interrupted his pacing. With his boss nowhere in sight, he figured he could use the distraction. He walked over to the main desk and smiled at Buddy.

"What's up?"

"Application, can you do a quick look and see? We are running out of time in filling Mel's position. Just remember, the new hire needs to be able to work with kids."

Mathias shrugged and walked back to the classrooms. He put on a smile and walked into the room.

"Hi, can I help you?"

His brain had a hard time reconciling seeing Siona in his office space. She held out papers toward him.

"I would like to apply for a job please?" she said. "I'm an out of work research astrophysicist, relocating for school. I've learned that Flint is home to the most modern planetarium facility in America from what I hear. It has 129 seats, and the 52 inch dome is complete with overlapping screens and a sloped floor to immerse visitors in the imagery of the planetarium's new Digistar 5 projection system. It turns planetariums into virtual-reality theaters and lets the audiences fly out among the planets and in the galaxy."

"Siona? What are you doing here?"

"In addition to my years of experience at the Hayden planetarium in New York, I've brought my resume and a few letters of recommendation," she said, against holding out the papers toward him.

"What are you doing here?" Mathias stuttered.

"I am here applying for a job."

"Why?"

"Because I like to eat. My job as a Teaching Assistant is great, but I'm doing to need a little something on the side," she said with a grin and waved the sheaf in her hand. "Can you at least look over my resume?"

"You're moving here?"

"I love how quick on your feet you are," she laughed. "Oh wait, I suppose I shouldn't insult my soon to be boss."

"You can't be here. I was going to move out to you. I already made the plans."

"What? Mathias what are you talking about?"

Mathias enjoyed the look of surprise on her face; it put them on equal footing.

"I have a meeting with Todd in a few minutes, to ask him for a reference for the Hayden. I talked to Marcus and he was going to go with me to Central Park. We were going to make sure there wasn't a problem with me being in the area. I was getting ready to find an apartment and everything. What are you doing here? Wait, you are really moving out here to be with me?"

"Well kinda," she said. "My parents decided to move here to be closer to family. I also got accepted into the Astrophysics program at the University of Flint. It seemed a lot like kismet."

Mathias pulled her into a kiss. While they had promised to try a long distance relationship, he had found it hard. He wanted to be with her, not just hear her voice on the phone. Their embrace broke and he hugged her tightly to him. He had never expected her to want to move.

"Those are some pretty good reasons," he said.

"They are okay reasons," she grinned. "I have a boyfriend that lives here too."

"Lucky," Mathias smiled.

"Yes, we are."

He grabbed her hand and kissed it.

"So about that job?"

"Can you work with kids?"

"I can try. If nothing else, we will make a lot of homemade telescopes."

"You're hired. Let me give you a tour. Oh, there's one more thing."

He winked at her quizzical expression.

"I would like you to come and meet my family.

About The STEAM Series

Dear Readers,

Most of you have heard of the STEM subjects- Science—Technology—Engineering—Mathematics.

However there has been a push from those in The Arts and Humanities to remember that arts and creativity are part of the process that makes things go. While educationally encouraging more women to explore the STEM subject is a great start, the critical process of creativity and innovation is missing.

STEAM is an educational approach to learning that uses Science, Technology, Engineering, the Arts and Mathematics as starting guide for and critical thinking.

I chose to highlight this, because you will find the women in this series, to be smart and savvy in their fields, but definitely creative when it comes to living a world where the paranormal is real.

Happy Reading!

JFF

About the Author

Jennifer Fisch- Ferguson has been writing and publishing fantasy stories since 2003. Publishing credits include writing contests and self-published novels and two separate series under consideration by agents.

She attended the Eastern Michigan University and graduated with a B.A in African American History and promptly went to work with AmeriCorps on a literary initiative. She went to the University of Michigan and got her Master's degree in Public Administration in 2008 and while she finished writing her thesis, also got a Masters in English – Composition and Rhetoric in 2009. She received her PhD at Michigan State University in the field of Professional Writing and Digital Rhetorics. She has been teaching collegiate and community writing classes since 2003 and loves the variety and inspiration her students bring.

She writes urban fantasy, paranormal romance, and young adult urban fantasy. She is excitedly expanding her ever developing world and looks forward to the new adventures waiting to be written.

See more at:

AuthorJFF.com

https://www.facebook.com/ETM.JFF

Sneak Peek· The STEAM Series Book 3

Wish Upon a Starr

Chapter One

Chris Starr pushed the accelerator and tightened her thigh muscles as the snowmobile leapt forward. Snow spattered against her goggles as she leaned forward and to the left to make the turn. The sled jumped, banking hard, but she kept tight control of the machine. Opening up the throttle and let the engine showcase its power; she rode a few minutes longer and then pressed the brake. A clicking noise caught her ear; she frowned in irritation as the bike slowed smoothly under her. She slammed down on the pedal, preparing her body for the jerking motion, and frowned as it stuttered and clicked more before it came to a harsh snow spitting stop.

Even though the brakes engaged just fine, the noise pissed her off. After the amount of time the bike had spent in the garage under her direct attention, she expected the brakes to be flawless, not clicking. Chris started the engine again and after riding a few minutes pressed the pedal again. And heard another click.

"Dammit," she said blowing a frustrated cloud of steam into the air.

Riding back to the parking lot, where her truck and trailer sat. Chris loaded the machine and secured it before hopping off the trailer. She grabbed a notebook from her truck and wrote down her observation notes before they left her memory and sighed. She began poking at the braking system and scowled. There was no reason for her bike to have made that noise. Her phone rang, scaring her into a shriek dissolving into laughing at her own reaction as she pressed the talk icon.

"Hey, Mom," she said. "You almost gave me a heart attack."

"Biology works quite differently, Dearest," her mother grumbled.

"And this is why I'm an engineer. Obviously biology doesn't make sense to me," Chris grumbled. "What has you up this early in the morning? Is everything okay?"

"Everything is just fine. My only child is in town. I thought we could have breakfast before I go to work."

Chris smiled at the phone and made plans to meet her mother in thirty minutes. She didn't begrudge her mother wanting to spend time together. It had been almost two years since she had been home last. Not to mention, food sounded good. While she had a weekly phone date with her parents, it just wasn't the same as seeing them in person. She double checked to make sure she had locked down the snowmobile securely and left Richfield Park. Despite having good riding trails, it was fairly empty; then again it was a weekday. Not everyone got to ride snowmobiles for a living.

She pulled into her parent's driveway fifteen minutes later. She almost made it to the door before twin bundles of fluffy excitement tackled her. PSR J0737−3039A and PSR J0737−3039B were bigger than she imagined they would be after only having seen pictures. Chris laughed and tried to push the puppies away, but at ninety pounds each, the wriggling, squirming and sloppy tongue kiss giving malamutes won and she fell back in the snow. As she wrestled and hugged the bundles of joy, a gruff bark stopped the play.

"Come here, you old spoil sport," Chris said with affection. "I'm not ignoring you. I've only seen pictures of the twins. Surely you can't be jealous."

Chris rolled her eyes at the short series of barks and huffs coming from the doorway.

"Fine, I will come in and pet you. Lazy Mama," she said in gentle admonishment. "Come on 3039A and 3039B."

The puppies tripped over each other as they bound into the house, running over her feet as she shook her head at the exuberance. When the hallway cleared, the older dog came over to her. Chris's heart broke a small bit to see her moving more slowly and carefully than she had a few years ago. She knew SN1604 was almost eleven years old, but still didn't want to think of her dog leaving. She bent down and spoke nonsensical loving words as she scratched and petted her. Once the dog had enough affection and walked away, Chris shucked off her winter gear. She heard bustling in the kitchen and shook her head. The click still haunted her ears.

"Hi, Dad," she said as she walked into the kitchen.

Her father turned to smile at her and Chris gave him a long tight hug. She pulled back and smiled at him. Her father looked a bit older too. She made a mental to note to get home much more often.

"She conned you into making French toast?"

"She said the magic words," her father chuckled.

"Mom said please?" Chris raising her eyebrows in over dramatic surprise.

"Of course not. Your mother never says 'please'," her father laughed. "She said 'Chris is home'."

"Wow, she played dirty pool didn't she?"

"*She* is strategic and calculating," her mother sniffed, walking into the kitchen. "You got your math skills from both of us, no matter what *he* thinks."

Chris went and hugged her mother. When the slight woman pushed her away to grab a coffee mug they all laughed.

"We could have met at a restaurant," she said. "No need to make Dad wake up early and cook food."

Her mother snorted and rolled her eyes.

"Did Dad forget he teaches engineering, again?" she asked in mock surprise. "Or did he finally get the degree in food science he's been dreaming about for so long."

"Your father has been watching his documentaries again. We no longer can eat high fructose corn syrup or any artificial sweeteners. Restaurants are out. And I'll kill him if he talks about getting another degree again."

Chris accepted a steaming mug of coffee from her father, who rolled his eyes and continued to laugh under his breath, before joining her mother at the booth in the breakfast nook.

She relaxed and enjoyed being with her parents. Even though she loved her work and was completely at ease and comfortable in her condo, coming home was always an amazing experience. Every time. She embraced the silence as her mother finished her first mug of coffee. Her dad came by with warm ups and she winked at him.

"Breakfast will be ready in about four minutes. I want you to try this new spice blend I created for the scrambled eggs," her dad said.

"Salt and pepper. That's all I need. I was raised to be a simple girl."

Her mother snorted from deep in her mug, as she continued drinking. Her father gave her a scathing look over his shoulder.

"But of course, you are the cook, and I will try whatever you set in front of me," Chris grinned, holding her hands up in surrender. "Mother, someday you're going to inhale and choke on coffee from being snide."

"If they made coffee snortable it would be the drug of my choice," her mother replied. "And when over the rainbow, did you become so accommodating?"

Her dad slid a platter on the table. Chris's mouth watered at the sight of French toast, bacon and eggs.

"You get a ten for plating."

"Suck up," her mother taunted her in a whisper.

"Am not," she mock-hissed back. "And your cursing needs work."

Chris took an exaggeratedly huge bite of food. She closed her eyes as the flavors warmed her. After giving her dad a thumbs up, she sat back and waited for him to join them at the nook. They ate in silence for a few moments.

"Did it pop or click?" her dad asked.

She ignored the knowing look her mother tossed her way and made it a point of eating a strip of bacon before answering.

"Clicked. I opened up the throttle full. When I rounded a corner, my brakes have the nerve to make a sound," she sighed in disgust. "Thankfully it doesn't need to be ready for the race this weekend. But still the darn thing shouldn't click."

She finished, refilled her plate with more French toast, and began to enjoy again. Her father was as precise in cooking as he was with equations. Each syrupy delicious bite prompted her to eat least two more pieces of toast than she needed. A woof from her left reminded her she'd been remiss. She held a piece of bacon down as a peace offering.

"*Christmas,*" her mother admonished. "You know she doesn't need all that fat. The vet said SN1604 is supposed to lose fifteen pounds."

"Super Novas are supposed to be big," she said, petting the dog. "Besides, at eleven, I think it's too late for her to break her bacon addiction."

She grinned at her Mom and fed the puppies a piece of bacon too, for good measure.

"If you want to load her up in the garage, I'll take a look. I don't have class until two this afternoon."

"Okay, sounds great. I'll help Mom clean up and then meet you out there in an hour," she said and then interrupted her dad as he open his mouth to speak. "And no, I won't touch your cast iron skillets. Even though I know full well they are supposed to be salt scrubbed and not touched with soap. Also to pat them dry and add a layer of lard to keep the seasoning."

She collected the plates and made her way to the sink as her parents laughed at her. She muttered, just loud enough, about the perils of being an only child to two overly affectionate parents. Her mother joined her at the sink and they managed to get half way through the dishes before soapy sponges were being tossed. Chris got in one sponge to land on her mother's chest and was rewarded with a sponge to the eye.

"You better dry off and go out in the garage before Dad remodels your bike," her mother warned.

"He wouldn't dare," she grinned. "He's afraid I might cry."

"And you said I play dirty pool," her mother scoffed. "I have never used my feminine wiles on him."

Chris burst out laughing at the proclamation.

197

"Feminine. Wiles. You do know what *wiles* means…"

A sponge landed in her open mouth and she gagged on the soap. She blew a raspberry at her mother, but behaved until they quickly finished the dishes.

"I am female darling, you should know at least that much biology."

"You are female, of course, but despite your pitiful attempt at being a free loving hippie – you have zero idea of how to flirt. You've never mastered those calculations."

"I've never had to," her mother proclaimed. "Men fell over themselves because of my brilliance."

"Or your double D's."

Chris side stepped the sponge thrown at her and made her way out to the garage. Her dad already had her bike on the lift and was peering at the braking system.

"Looks like the nut and bolt holding your lever are sticking between the lever and bracket itself."

She nodded at her dad and pointed out the vexing area. Her dad smiled at her and she knew he waited for an answer.

"Yes, I removed, flushed and replaced the fluid. That's a beginner move."

"No air bubbles?"

"Funny, Dad. Of course I checked for them. I think the caliper piston is over-traveled. But since the pistons move at the same time, it might also be a warped rotor, meaning hot brake fluid."

Chris spent thirty more minutes with her dad looking for the problem. The frustrating part was she had created the braking system inside and out. The issue was bound to be something small and overlooked and it make her want to throw her wrench. In the end, they found the master cylinder wasn't releasing the pressure on the caliper. Even though her dad said nothing, Chris knew he hid a smile. She had overlooked an obvious issue. Together they fixed it in twenty minutes and she walked back in to spend more quality time with her family.

A few hours later, her parents were on their way to the University of Flint, where they were full tenured professors. She had promised she would stop by and say hello to her parent's friends. She also had plans to stop by and see her old professors, but first, she needed to get her newly modified bike back out on the trails. Even though they had fixed the problem, she had a gut feeling there was more to the problem. If she banked too hard, it still acted up.

She drove back out to the park and found the parking lot near the first pavilion fairly empty. Chris smiled at the thought of how many adults should have called in sick to ride the trails before the snow got packed down. The conditions were great for riding and she couldn't imagine missing such an opportunity. She unloaded her bike, adjusted her gear and seat, and took off. She listened intently as the gears shifted when she moved into a faster speed. She smiled as the braking system moved through smoothly. No hints of the clicking that had plagued her earlier. She opened up the throttle and let the machine go.

She lost herself in the smooth ride and for a few moments was able to forget about all the moving parts and just enjoy it. Until another rider sped past her, whipped through a sharp turn kicking snow back at her. She did a double take. It looked like one of her bikes, but she couldn't identify it immediately which bothered her.

"What the…"

The stream of curse words flowing from her mouth would have made her mother proud. She kept up a running monologue until she rounded the final two corners. Where her bike and the obnoxious rider sat. She slowed as she drew closer, not sure how she should approach him, even if she should approach him, but she needed to figure out which model he rode. She stopped and took off her helmet.

"I thought you were a dude," the guy said as he removed his own helmet. "You ride wicked fast. I was gonna offer you a beer for dusting you."

"Because only guys can ride a snowmobile?" she asked. "Women drink beer too, just not the cheap crap."

Chris was trying to get her stupefied hormones under control. It wasn't enough the guy could ride well and rode her bike, but he also was gorgeous. Seconds later his good looks and sexy smile were overshadowed by his condescending attitude.

"Everyone looks the same in all the gear," he said. "But most of the time the riders are guys."

She tried to stop her eyebrow from rising, but it did. She just stared at him and to her astonishment; he met her gaze and stared back. Chris was used to people lowering their gaze when she held eye contact. It appeared to be a contest of the wills, and she wasn't used to failing. Instead she took the time to look him over. He was about six three, even though he sat, he was sitting on her bike and she knew its dimensions by heart. He had medium brown skin, maybe a few shades lighter than her own mocha color. He had freckles over his cheeks, which were damningly appealing and eyes that resembled thick pools of molasses.

"Like what you see?"

The trance cast by his eye color was broken. He'd blinked and she won.

"Yes, I really do," she purred. Chris climbed off her bike and walked over to him. She ran a hand over the handles of her bike. She leaned in close. "This is a gorgeous bike."

She winked at him and tuned back to her own bike. She made space between them before she ran a hand over his thighs. He was riding the newest model. The one that hadn't been commercially released yet. All of a sudden she knew exactly who he was.

"Don't I even get a name?" he asked.

"You parents didn't give you one?

She didn't bother to look back over her shoulder as she returned to her snowmobile.

"Nathaniel," he chuckled. "Will you tell me yours?"

"Chris."

"Well, Chris, glad my sled is so pleasing to you."

She bit her tongue so she wouldn't have to correct him. She actually wanted to see him in action.

"Can you actually ride it? I mean, it's premium with a lot of power," she taunted.

"Sounds like you might want a race," he said. "I'm up for a race, as long as you don't expect me to throw it because you are a beautiful woman."

The fluttering in her stomach made her mentally scold herself. She shouldn't be affected by a clearly well used line he gave her as a compliment.

"I would never expect you to throw a race," she grinned. "But don't expect me to go easy just because you're flirting with me."

Chris smirked as Nathaniel turned up the wattage on his smile.

"I think, just to keep things above board, we should make a bet."

"What kind of bet?" she asked.

"The loser should buy drinks," he said.

"It's eleven in the morning," she scoffed.

"It's five somewhere in the world," he said.

"Great old tired line," Chris snorted

"Are you afraid you will lose?" he mocked.

Chris just shook her head and pulled her helmet back on. She hoped she would lose to him, if not she would have to fire him.